# CHILD
# BRIDE

# CHILD BRIDE

A Novel

JENNIFER SMITH TURNER

Published by SparkPress, a BookSparks imprint,
A division of SparkPoint Studio, LLC
Phoenix, Arizona, USA, 85007
www.gosparkpress.com

Published 2019
Printed in the United States of America
ISBN: 978-1-68463-038-7 (pbk)
ISBN: 978-1-68463-039-4 (ebk)
Library of Congress Control Number: 2019911285

*Book Design by Stacey Aaronson*

*Dedicated to my best friend, the love of my life.*
*Eric, you make all things possible.*

# Chapter One

MY CHILDHOOD FARM IN LOUISIANA WASN'T MUCH TO look at. It stood on a long, dusty road, one of many small hog and pecan farms owned and worked by the descendants of sharecroppers and former slaves. Our house had been built by hand; the wood shingles were uneven, the doors never closed completely, and the window frames were crooked. Ninety-degree angles didn't find a home in this house. We had a few pictures hanging on the wall right by the front door near a window. One was of my grandparents, my daddy's parents. The image was murky, all dark and grainy, as if the camera needed a better focus on their faces. My grandparents stood shoulder to shoulder in the picture, their bodies framed in an oval cutout. Their eyes looked straight ahead, staring into the camera and at me whenever I was close to the picture. There were no smiles or grins on their faces. It was as though they were angry, unhappy, or tired—weary like my daddy sometimes looked when he came in from the fields. Grandma's hair was pulled back in a tight bun with a straight part down the middle of her head. Grandpa had hair all over his face, a thick mustache and long beard that looked rugged and wiry, like the steel wool in the kitchen Momma used to clean pots and pans. My daddy looked a lot like his daddy.

Every time Daddy walked past their picture, he'd give

the frame a little nudge to straighten it. But it never seemed to work. If the frame was parallel to the doorframe, it was crooked to the window casing. And when it lined up with the angle of the window, it was lopsided to the doorframe. The few times the picture actually looked straight, with my grandparents' eyes level with my daddy's eyes, both the door and window seemed to slope to one side. I took to just tilting my head left or right to look at the picture—seemed to be easier. But Daddy always touched the frame.

We didn't have a picture of my momma's parents on the wall. She kept their picture in the drawer of the nightstand by the bed. Sometimes I'd see her holding the picture, stroking the glass on the frame. I asked her once why her parents' picture wasn't on the wall. She looked sad and said, "I like to have them close to me at night."

The sweeping front porch was the best part of the house. There we'd spend hot evenings waiting for the slightest breeze to move the heavy Louisiana air in hopes of a moment of coolness. We children would grab our pillows and sheets, lay our bodies on the porch for the night, giggle and tease one another. Stretched out on our backs, hands behind our heads, faces turned to the heavens, we'd count the stars and hope to see the tail of a shooting star make its way across the sky. One time, Robert, the oldest, stayed a while with us and explained the different star formations. "See that, over there? That's the North Star. It's the brightest star in the sky." He pointed up, and our eyes followed the angle of his finger. "If you start at the North Star you can outline the Little Dipper. The North Star is the tip of the handle. See there, the brightest star? And the ladle part is connected, like the ladle we use to scoop water at the well."

"Robert," I asked, "how do you know about stars and the sky?"

He lay still for moment, his head tilted all the way back, as if he were letting sunshine soak into his skin. "Once I dreamed I'd learned everything about the sky and stars— how it all came to be, what the proper names are for each star and planet. I wanted to be a learned man, know more than just farm-and-fields knowing. But schooling wasn't meant for me, or me for it."

He fell silent again, rubbed his forehead, and went inside, leaving us, the little ones, to guess at the stars' names for ourselves. The crickets and cicadas provided background sounds to our astral explorations. And then the fireflies began their light dance, bringing the stars even closer to us. We reveled in our sanctuary—until the mosquitoes and flies forced us back inside.

The other family gathering place was the kitchen. Food was cleaned, prepared, eaten, and stored there. It was the largest room of the house, the place where my momma spent most of her time. Momma taught me how to measure seasonings at the kitchen counter that my daddy and brothers had built. "Just a pinch of salt; soon you'll know what a pinch feels like," she'd say. I watched her pinch seasoning from the palm of her hand, her fingertips becoming measuring tools.

One day Momma told me to make the breakfast biscuits by myself. "I can help you if you need me," she said. I got the ingredients from the food cabinet and icebox—flour, baking soda, yeast, sugar, salt, eggs, butter, and milk. I arranged everything on the counter, placed the mixing bowl in the center, and grabbed the tools I needed to make the biscuits. I looked at Momma. "Do I have it right so far?" She nodded her head and went about making the breakfast meat and eggs. I folded the dry stuff together just the way Momma had shown me. Then I added the eggs, butter, and liquids and stirred using a fork. Dough started to form. I thought the mixture was ready to be pressed into lumps and go onto the baking sheet. "Is this ready, Momma?"

"You the cook, you decide," she said as she turned the bacon over. But just as I was about to put the first mound of dough on the baking sheet Momma coughed and said, "Best to grease the sheet—that way the biscuits won't stick to the pan. It's also good to put food in a hot oven."

I took a stick of butter and ran it across the baking sheet, leaving thick clumps everywhere. The matches for the oven were sitting on the counter next to Momma. She stepped aside so I could get them and open the oven door. The only other time I'd lit the oven Momma had let me strike the match, but she'd put it into the pilot light to start the flame, while I worked the oven dial. I looked up at her now, to see if she was going to help, but she didn't turn my way. I tried to strike the match, but nothing happened. I tried again—nothing. On my next try the match lit and broke at the same time, causing a flame to fall to the floor. I jumped back and stomped my foot on the tiny fire.

"Momma, I need help," I cried out to her.

"A cook got to know how to strike a match and light an oven. Try again."

This time the match lit on the first strike. I placed it in the opening for the oven and turned the temperature dial as far as it would go to the right. To my young eyes, it seemed as though I were responsible for starting a bonfire, with the blue and white-tipped flames dancing in the wind. I stepped back, closed the oven door. Momma slid to her spot in front of the stove.

I was able to cut the dough into twenty biscuits; some were smaller than others and some looked a little funny, but there was more than enough for everyone. "Momma. I'm ready to put this in the oven. Don't they look good?" I tilted the baking sheet so Momma could admire my work.

"Is the oven at the right temperature?" she responded as she examined the collection of dough.

"What's the right temperature?"

"The temperature that will cook the biscuits without burning them or leaving the dough in the middle uncooked."

"How am I supposed to know?"

"Baby Girl, you've been watching me make biscuits every morning since you could walk and talk on your own. You've seen how I work the oven. What've you learned?"

Momma turned the dial to the left, making a half circle of the full circle I'd made earlier. "This is the correct setting. At the very top where you put the dial, is the hottest. You can roast a pig at that setting—too hot for biscuits. Now you have to wait and let it cool down before you put the biscuits in, or they'll just burn."

That morning Daddy, my brother Robert, his wife, Bernice, and two of my middle brothers would eat first. The men had been working the farm since sunrise, as they did most every day—except Sunday, when we all went to church to celebrate and thank the Lord for our blessings. The men took turns in the fields, then came to eat in shifts before heading back out to the fields until dinnertime. I was happy that Daddy was going to have my biscuits when I took them straight out of the oven—still hot and moist, the butter melted and dripping. The men on the next shift would have cold biscuits, whatever was left from the first group who had already eaten.

I watched everyone take their seats at the table. Daddy sat at the head, facing the door to the porch, Momma sat at his right, my brother Robert sat at the other end, facing Daddy, and Bernice sat to Robert's right. Everyone else filled in wherever there was an empty chair.

I wanted to push the biscuits directly in front of Daddy, but Momma had a certain spot for each food platter on the table. The breakfast meats—bacon, sausage, and ham hocks —were placed closest to Daddy. The scrambled eggs came next, then the biscuits. Pancakes and hot oatmeal followed, along with the seasonings—salt, pepper, maple syrup, and sugar. Jugs of milk, orange juice, and water filled in the corners of the table.

Daddy blessed the food. I kept one eye open during the blessing.

"Baby Girl made these biscuits all by herself," Momma announced after the blessings were said and Daddy started to fill his plate.

"Think I'll start with a biscuit." Daddy reached for the biscuit plate. I helped, holding the platter out to him.

"I'll start there too," Robert chimed in. "Pass those down here."

The platter was passed down the table, and everyone took a biscuit. I watched as Daddy brought the biscuit to his lips. He took a big bite. Suddenly he stopped. He looked over at Momma. She took a small bite from her biscuit. She stopped too. Robert put his down on his plate and began drinking water. The younger brothers screamed. They looked as if they wanted to spit the food on the floor. "Don't you dare spit at the table!" Momma scolded them as she grabbed a glass of water. Daddy had already finished drinking his water and was pouring himself more. Bernice nibbled at her biscuit and said, "Think I'll have some water too."

No one looked at me. I grabbed a biscuit and took a big bite. My mouth began to sting in the corners by my jaw. I wanted to spit out the biscuit, but I took a big swallow, acting as though I actually liked what I was eating. But all I could taste was salt, as if I had held the salt shaker up to my mouth and poured salt onto my tongue. I gulped down my water and rubbed tears from the corner of my eyes.

When we were cleaning up, Momma asked, "Baby Girl, did you taste your food while you were cooking?"

"Momma, you knew I made a mistake. Why didn't you say something?"

"The only way to learn is from mistakes. Close your eyes and hold out your hand." Momma poured something into my hand. "Now take your other hand and gently rub your fingers over this. Make small circles in your palm."

I did as she told me, slowly rubbing the stuff.

"What does it feel like?" she asked.

"Soft but gritty."

"Does it have a smell?"

I held my palm up to my nose. "Not that I can tell."

"Now wipe your hand clean, and I'm gonna put something else in your palm." She poured something into my hand again. "Now rub this the same way with your fingers. Does this feel different?"

"It's softer, not as gritty."

"Does this have a smell?"

I tried again but still didn't smell anything.

"But it does feel different?"

"Yes."

"Now open your eyes."

The salt and sugar containers were sitting on the table in front of me. The containers looked exactly the same—silver tins with tops that had to be twisted off. I'd struggled to open one of the tins when I was making the biscuits. I remembered I'd put it down to get something to pry it open with. The salt went in the mixture first, then sugar, but that was the tin I'd struggled with. The tins were next to each other.

"A cook needs to understand the feel of ingredients," Momma said. "Touch is everything to good cooking."

"But the salt and sugar don't feel that different. Wouldn't it be easier just to use different-looking containers?"

"Baby Girl, you sassing me?"

"I'm sorry, Momma. Guess I should throw these out before the others come in for breakfast." I reached for the biscuits to toss them into the trash.

"You'll do no such thing! We don't waste food here."

"But they're terrible."

"Time for another lesson. Get the butter, milk, a bowl, and the sugar."

I scurried around, collecting the items, and placed them all on the counter.

"The oven is still warm," she said. "Put the butter in, so it will be soft enough to mix. Pour the sugar in the bowl—don't be shy, use a lot, at least a full cup."

I measured out a cup and dumped it into the bowl.

"Pour the milk in and then add the butter; it should be soft now. And then fold the butter into the milk and sugar." I worked the soft butter into the milk and sugar, pressing the fork down with each turn of my hand. "Keep adding milk until the mixture is smooth, so it can be spread on the biscuits. And taste it as you go, make sure it's very sweet. Add more sugar if you need to." Momma began to arrange the biscuits on the baking dish. "Baby Girl, use the basting brush and spread the sugar mixture on each biscuit. We'll put the biscuits back in the oven and let them stay warm for the next breakfast seating. But sprinkle some sugar on top, just to be sure—too sweet is never a problem."

DADDY WAS ALWAYS working the farm. His coveralls were smeared with mud after he cleaned the slop out of the hog pen. He made my brothers work with him. Everyone hated this task. The hogs were mean animals, always snorting. They looked as though they'd attack at any moment. And they stank. Whoever had to clean the pen smelled for days after; only time could erase the stench. Daddy was never afraid of anything. He didn't even seem to mind the smell. "These animals keep us fed, that's all that matters," he'd say.

I could hear his voice as he sat on the porch talking with the other men. He listened more than he talked. The other men told jokes, stories about the day's activity on the farm, the goings-on with their families. When Daddy spoke, every word was deliberate and punctuated with his deep voice. He gave advice to the others, and they listened intently to whatever he said.

Occasionally it would be just him and me on the porch.

Once he taught me how to handle a pocket knife. "Come here, Baby Girl, time you learned how to do this." He used his knife to whittle pieces of wood. He would make smoking pipes or stick figures that we got to play with. He could peel an entire apple with one long piece of skin falling to the floor before he began to cut the apple in pieces and eat from his knife.

"This is how you hold the knife and the apple to peel it." He held the knife in his hand to show me the angle, then placed the apple in my hand. "There, now you try."

In his hand the apple was small, just sitting in the hollow of his palm; I could barely get my fingers around it. "I can't hold it, Daddy. It's too big. You do it for me." I handed the apple back.

"No, you have to try." He folded my tiny hand around the apple, made the first cut on the skin with the knife, and told me to finish.

I held onto the knife and apple as best I could, but the knife slipped right away and cut the tip of my thumb.

Daddy looked and said, "It's just a small nick—keep going."

My blood began to spill onto the apple. I got scared, but I didn't want to cry or stop. I ignored the blood that was turning the apple meat pink and continued making my way around the apple with the knife. One long piece of skin started to dangle from the apple. "Look, Daddy, I'm doing it!"

The curve of the wood handle on the knife had indentations from where my daddy wrapped his fingers around it. I used these spots to grip tighter, to steady the blade. I could feel the carvings in the handle press against my skin. My hand was shaking and getting wet from sweat and apple juice. The apple skin pieces were getting smaller and smaller. I looked up at Daddy.

"Keep going, you're almost there," Daddy said.

I kept at it—there wasn't much skin left on the apple. "I did it, one piece of skin," I said finally as the peel fell to the ground. "I did it, just like you."

"Very good. Now I'll show you how to eat from the knife." He took the apple in his hand. "Here—you make a small slice, but don't cut it all the way. You don't want to prick your thumb again. Then you fold the slice and hold it between the knife and your thumb, and you eat it from the dull side of the knife, like this." He slipped the apple wedge into his mouth. Then he put the apple back in my hand.

DADDY WAS CALLED "Mr. Jones" by everyone in our small but large county—not many people, and miles between each home. I knew the names of every farmer on the long road that led from our farm to the main street in town. It was a narrow road, filled with dust, rocks, and ruts made by the trucks and farm equipment that lumbered up and down all day. The road was lined with cotton and corn fields on both sides and sprinkled with pecan trees, almost like a grand boulevard in a big city. At least I liked to think it looked that way, whenever I walked to school or town.

I recall one time walking with Daddy to the store in town to pick up some provisions. It was a warm day, and Daddy told me to come with him and walk rather than ride up the road in the truck. "We'll just walk, enjoy the day, and say hello to neighbors along the way," he said.

Daddy had a long stride, with legs that made up most of

his tall height, so I had to move my legs quickly just to keep at his side. Whenever we came upon a good-sized rock I'd kick it down the road, run in front of Daddy to where it landed, and then kick it again.

As we passed our neighbors' farms, the families would wave and shout, "Hello, Mr. Jones, nice day." Daddy and I would wave back and continue on our way. We stopped at one neighbor's porch, as everyone was sitting outside, and chatted for a while. I was able to visit with my school friends while Daddy talked to the men on the porch. They spoke in hushed whispers. Something had happened that upset the grown-ups. The night before, I had heard my parents speaking in the same quiet voices, with a sense of urgency, or maybe it was fear.

When Daddy was finished visiting, we continued walking the last mile to the general store. He was silent for the rest of our walk. I looked up at him a couple of times, but he didn't look my way. The wrinkles on his forehead and the blood vessels at his temple stood out large and firm. As we approached the steps to the store I saw a crowd of people on the steps, the porch, and inside the store. They were white, every one of them.

Daddy put his hand on my shoulder, signaling for me to slow down and stay close by his side. He took his cap off and placed it in the back pocket of his coveralls. Then he wiped his brow with his handkerchief. He rubbed the dust off his shoes on the back of his pant legs, and with his eyes cast down he led me up the steps into the store.

People made a space for us to enter, but it was a small space, only wide enough for one tiny person to pass without touching bodies on either side. We crept sideways through them. As I peeked up I could see that their faces were pressed tight, as if they were sucking on sour lemon drops. They smelled too, like the sweat stink lingering on dirty work clothes or a wet dog. I held my nose. Daddy nudged me to keep my face down.

"What you want, boy?" the shopkeeper said in an angry tone to Daddy.

"I need some flour, milk, and a few other things, sir, just some things for the wife. The cupboards are getting bare." Daddy answered without making eye contact. He looked down at the tips of his shoes, his clean shoes.

"This ain't a good time. You need to go." The man looked at the other people and waved his hand at Daddy as though he were a mosquito. "Git out, boy. You don't belong here now, git out!" As he raised his voice the other people began to close in on us, creating even more tightness in the space between them and us.

"Yes, sir," Daddy said. He began backing out of the store, holding me tight at his side but pushing me toward the steps. I nearly fell off the top step before we turned around and walked forward.

At the bottom there were three girls in cute dresses, hair pulled back in pigtails with big bows made from fancy pink and yellow ribbons. They stuck their tongues out at me and made hissing noises in my face. I could smell their breath, laced with the scent of chocolate and sugar. I knew better than to look them in the eye or stick my tongue out at them, but I wanted to. That was the closest I'd ever been to white girls.

"Come on, Baby Girl, let's go home." Daddy began walking down the road. He didn't take my hand. His shoulders sloped down, and his stride was slower, as though he had just worked in the fields all day. He kept his head down.

I reached up and took his hand. "It'll be okay, Daddy," I said. "Momma and I can find something to cook tonight." I was shaking all over, and I felt trembling in his hand too. His palm was wet from sweat. I held on tighter.

When we approached our neighbor's farm they shouted out hello again and called Daddy "Mr. Jones." Seemed like this made him walk taller, less tired-looking.

Finally I asked him, "What happened, Daddy? What have all the grown-ups been talking about? The whites too."

He didn't say anything at first, but then he stopped and said, "A boy was killed, Baby Girl. They killed him."

"Why?"

He started walking again, shaking his head from side to side. "The boy whistled at a woman. That's all he did. She was a white woman. They said he whistled at her in a store in Mississippi."

"He was a colored boy?" I asked.

"Just fourteen years old." Daddy's voice trailed off; it felt as if I'd lost him again. "He was from the North—Chicago. He was just visiting."

"Fourteen! Kids in my class are that age."

"I know, Baby Girl. He's the same age as your friends." He rubbed my cheek as he said this and looked deep into my eyes. His eyes looked as sad as when my granddaddy died.

As our farm came into sight Daddy began to walk faster, with a lighter step. The family was out on the porch, and right away they noticed we didn't have any food with us.

"Where's our food?" Momma asked impatiently, but she stopped when she saw the look on my daddy's face.

"Crowd at the general store. We'll shop another time," Daddy mumbled. He took his handkerchief out and dusted off his shoes. "Guess I'll go clean and polish these. Kicked up a lot of dust on that walk." He disappeared inside.

Momma took hold of me and gave me a strong hug. She held onto me, rocking back and forth and humming her favorite church hymn. When she let go, she held me by the shoulders and stared at my face.

"What's wrong, Momma?"

She shook her head, pulled me close again. Then she let out a sigh and went inside.

I sat on the steps by myself, thinking about how strange grown-ups could be.

THE NEXT WEEK at school Miss Parker told us what had happened to Emmett Till—that was his name, the Northern boy who'd been killed for whistling at a white woman. She showed us the awful pictures of him that his family wanted everyone to see. I don't think our parents would have wanted us to see those images. But Miss Parker thought it was important that we understand the world around us. She said, "You children need to be careful, very careful."

We gasped at what we saw, how horribly he had been beaten. His body was no bigger than most of ours. His clothes, from what we could make out in the murky picture, looked like things the boys in our classroom might wear, but there were big dark spots all over them.

# Chapter Two

I WAS THE YOUNGEST OF TWELVE. WE WERE A homegrown crew of field hands—pecan-pickers, hog-pen cleaners, chicken-slaughterers, house-cleaners, and cooks. My momma was my life trainer. She and the other women in the house trained me to be a good, hardworking wife and mother. "Preparing you for the future," Momma always said. Unlike my older sisters and brothers, I didn't witness the frequent changes in my momma's body, as she moved from standing straight with a strong back to carrying a soft, round belly with a sore back and then returning to standing erect with a baby sucking at her breast. It must have seemed an endless cycle to her. Later it was a cycle I'd see in my sisters and the women my brothers brought home to live with us. Their wives, I was told. We weren't talkative people. Many things happened without words being spoken; looks and grunts often served as acknowledgment that a change had occurred or an event had taken place.

When a brother married and his wife moved into his sleeping space, a sister would leave our house to do the same at her new husband's home. The wife took my sister's place in the kitchen and began to look much like my momma, the wife's body changing as her posture labored with the weight of another life. On those rare occasions when one of my married sisters returned, she too would have the same full expectant body. There were full-bellied women everywhere. But I didn't want to be like them. It seemed there must be more to life than lying on your back for a man, getting a swelled belly, having a baby suck your nipple, and working away in the kitchen.

OUR SCHOOLHOUSE WAS a one-room building two miles from our farm. We always went to school in a group—my sisters, my brothers, friends from neighboring farms, and me. It was precious time away from the farm and our crowded house, time away from the oldest kids in the house and my parents. Although we were all different ages, the twenty children in the one-room school were taught by the only colored teacher in this part of the county. Miss Parker was my idol. Here was a woman who wore pretty clothes every day and shoes that fit her feet—no holes in the toes or straps that didn't cross the top of her foot completely. Her shoe buckles closed properly, and her dresses were always pressed. On Mondays she wore a dark blue dress with a little white lace collar. The dress had short sleeves, with a small button on the side of each. Tuesday was the flowered dress with a solid green collar and black buttons down the front. Wednesdays she wore a brown dress with elbow-length sleeves, a side zipper, and a thin belt. Then on Thursdays she'd have a black skirt on with a white blouse that had a little ribbon tied in a bow at her neck. Fridays she wore a dark blue skirt with a printed blouse.

Miss Parker often read aloud to us. *Cane*, by Jean

Toomer, was one of my favorites. I loved everything in the book, but my favorite poem was "Georgia Dusk." Miss Parker would start with the first stanza:

*The sky, lazily disdaining to pursue*
*The setting sun, too indolent to hold*
*A lengthened tournament for flashing gold,*
*Passively darkens for night's barbecue.*

When she asked us to read aloud, I was the only one in the class who ever volunteered. After pausing to see if any other student wanted to read, she'd call on me. "All right, Nell, please stand and read to the class." I'd stand and read the next stanza:

*A feast of moon and men and barking hounds,*
*An orgy for some genius of the South*
*With blood-hot eyes and cane-lipped scented mouth,*
*Surprised in making folk-songs from soul sounds.*

I'd pause and look at Miss Parker. She would nod and say, "Continue, Nell." I'd smile and go on. When I finished, I would take my seat and two other girls would stand to finish the reading. Listening to the beautiful words, mouthing them to myself as they read, feeling the words roll on my tongue, I felt I was in church, floating on currents of warm Southern air.

I OFTEN STAYED after school to help Miss Parker clean and prepare for the next day. Black chalkboards lined the wall at the front of the classroom. The letters of the alphabet hung above the boards on yellow heavy-duty paper, so old that the corners were frayed and browning. Each paper showed a capital letter, then a lower-case version, and then the cursive form. We practiced making the letters at our desks, using small copies of the alphabet chart. Before I cleaned the blackboards, I would write out the entire alphabet in longhand. "Very good, Nell," Miss Parker would say as she watched me write. "Not all the children can master cursive. But yours is quite nice, with a good flow to the letters."

Sometimes she would sit at her desk while I cleaned, in deep thought. I usually just went about cleaning, but one day I asked her if everything was okay.

"Nell, there's so much that I'd like to tell you children."

"Like what, Miss Parker?" I kept cleaning.

"It was nothing. I was just thinking out loud, Nell, that's all. You do such a good job helping me. Thank you."

"May I ask you something?"

"Of course."

"Do you have family? Were you ever married? Do you have children?"

"My, my. I do believe that is three questions, Nell."

"I'm sorry. Maybe just the first one, then. Do you have family?"

She smiled. "Why don't you sit for a while, and I'll tell you a little about myself."

I sat at my desk and folded my hands.

"I was like you once—a long time ago." She looked down at her hands, absently rubbing them together while pulling on one finger on her left hand. "I was born here. My daddy and momma were born here too. I think their parents, my grandparents, came from somewhere else, maybe deeper south or even from another part of the world. I never knew for sure. My parents never talked about my grandparents; they were probably slaves on some old farm. Sometimes old folk can't bring themselves to talk about things that hurt to the bone."

She drifted into silence, staring at the air with her arms folded across her chest as if she were giving herself a gentle hug. I remained quiet, my hands folded, and hoped she'd say more.

"I'm an only child, at least now I am. I had other siblings, but they didn't make it to adulthood. My parents are gone too. I'm a reader like you, Nell. My folks weren't educated, not in the formal book way. They were very smart, though. They knew everything about farming, growing crops, building, mending—anything that needed getting done, they could do. They taught me how to be self-sufficient. We didn't have books in our house, but one old lady from a neighboring farm had books she'd stolen. She told everyone that the missus had given her the books. No one believed her. It was illegal to teach slaves to read or write. Certainly there was no reason for a former slave to be given books. But that was her story. No one disagreed with her—not to her face, anyway. She'd visit our farm with her books, sit with me and any other children who were around, and read. She only had five books, and each was precious to her. *Jack and Jill: A Village Story* was my favorite."

"Why?" I asked.

"The author was Louisa May Alcott, a woman from up North. I liked that the story was set in a part of the world I knew nothing about, so I was learning about cold and snow.

And, I realize now, I liked that it was written by a woman. That mattered to me. To know that a woman could write stories and have them published, and that a slave-owner could own a book by such a writer—that was amazing. Later, when I learned more about who Louisa was—a Northerner whose family were abolitionists and well-educated—I felt a kinship to her in some strange way."

"Miss Parker, how'd you learn about her?"

"We have family up North, in Boston, where Louisa was from. I wrote to my cousin and asked if she knew anything about the Alcotts. She sent me all the information she could find at the library up there. There was quite a lot. Seems Louisa and her family have important history. But I was telling you about our neighbor, and how I got to reading books.

"The neighbor was a good reader, and she taught me how to read. Once I could read on my own, I read whatever I could find—food labels on cans and jars, information on sacks of flour, instructions that came with tools and farm equipment, bills that showed up in the mail, recipes my momma had written on little cards, the family bible, and church hymn books. We didn't have a school for coloreds then, but we always had church and Sunday School. I did most of my learning there."

Silence fell. I sat still for what seemed a long time and finally said, "Miss Parker. What happened to your family?"

"Speaking like this makes me remember. It's not always a good thing—remembering."

"I'm sorry, Miss Parker. I should go. Maybe we could talk again. I enjoyed listening to you." I stood up and started to gather my things. Then I heard her take a deep breath and let out a pain-filled sigh.

"They killed him—my daddy. Eventually they killed my momma, too, although in a different way."

"Miss Parker?" I stopped what I was doing and stood beside my desk.

She had her back to me, but I could see her wipe a tear from the corner of her eye. She reached into her pocket, took out a white lace handkerchief, and dabbed her nose. I sat sideways on the edge of my chair, waiting for her to speak. My heart was thumping a tune inside my chest, loud as the hammering noise my daddy and brothers made when fixing a fence.

Stillness and quiet were so foreign in the classroom. Usually I could hear the young ones giggling and laughing while they waved their hands in the air, asking if they could go pee. The older kids groaned at this, knowing that Miss Parker would assign someone to walk the little ones to the outhouse and wait. Once a boy had almost fallen through the hole. He yelled and screamed for help and was a mess after he was rescued. Miss Parker didn't allow the young ones to go alone after that. The rear of the classroom would dance with whispers and glances from the older kids. Notes written on tightly folded pieces of paper were slipped from hand to hand. The sound of pen knives carving the desk tops often distracted me from my silent reading. All the desks were left with etchings of initials and hearts—proclamations of young love.

Now, with just Miss Parker and me, I heard only quiet. Then she started to speak.

"It was late one night. We had finished supper and cleaned up. I remember the sky was filled with bright stars. I'd wanted to stay on the porch, stare up, and count them.

But Momma hustled me inside for bed. I was drifting off to sleep when loud noises woke me. Men on horses, wearing sheets with cutouts for their eyes, noses, and mouths, were circling our front porch. They shouted at Daddy, said he was a thief who had been tried and convicted. Now it was time for his sentencing. They took out a noose." Miss Parker stopped speaking and folded her arms more tightly. When she started again I didn't recognize her voice. Usually it was even in tone, gentle, almost soothing; now the voice I heard was deep, strong, filled with the harshness our preacher used whenever his sermon spoke about the work of the devil.

"My momma wailed for them to stop. She pleaded and begged on her knees. She crawled in the dirt at their horses' hooves. They spat on her. Told her to get out of the way, or else they could make a second noose. Momma was never the same after that night." Miss Parker stopped again, rubbed her stomach with one hand, and leaned against the wall with her fist clenched. I was afraid she might fall over or faint. She rested her head on her arm for a second, but then suddenly she stood tall, rolled her shoulders back, smoothed her hair, and took a deep breath. In the Miss Parker voice I recognized, she said, "Time for you to go home, Nell."

"Yes, Miss Parker." I rose and began to walk to the door, moving backward. "Ma'am?"

"Yes, Nell."

"I'm sorry about your daddy."

"Thank you. It's not something we'll talk about again."

"Yes, ma'am."

"Here, before you go—another book for you, *To Kill a Mockingbird*. I've shared this in class. The main character is a strong young girl called Scout. I think you'll relate to her. And take this too, for all your books."

She handed me a satchel. It was made from cloth that was faded with age and looked as if it had been a blanket at one time. The brown leather straps, stitched to each side, were worn smooth and had turned black in some spots, where fingers had found a steady home. A thin strip of cowhide was looped through a brass buckle to keep the bag closed, like a belt. Inside was one large section for books or papers, with a small zippered compartment for pencils. I sniffed the inside and smelled a thick aroma, full of history.

# Chapter Three

WHEN I TURNED FIFTEEN A NEW MAN BEGAN TO
visit the house. He'd sit on the front porch at least one
evening a week and drink iced tea with my daddy and brothers. Being a newcomer, he didn't say much except when he
rose to leave. Then he'd wipe the sweat of the humid summer night off his brow with a handkerchief and say, "Good
night." This went on right up to my sixteenth birthday—almost twelve months of being with the men-folk on the porch
without expressing an opinion of his own. After a while no
one took much notice of him; he was just there, part of the
assemblage passing the evening—until my sixteenth birthday.

That evening Momma had baked my favorite cake, dark
chocolate with white icing, and brought it out to the porch
with sixteen little wax candles shimmering on top. "This
here's a big day," Daddy said. "Sixteen means you're all
grown up now, my Baby Girl." He kissed me and gave me a
small gift wrapped in potato-sack cloth. "You can keep all
your special things in this."

I opened my gift to find a hand-carved box with my initials engraved on top. Inside were a pair of Momma's earrings. "You always playing with those," Momma said. "Time
you started to wear them as your own. You a woman now."

I was admiring my gift and eating cake when Henry, the newcomer, sat beside me on the porch step and said, "Happy birthday, Nell." His voice was a new musical vibration in my ears. Other men occasionally strung sentences together, but I never paid attention to what their voices sounded like. Hearing Henry's that evening caught me off guard. It was filled with a smooth, comforting, and inviting rhythm that welcomed me into its circle. "I have something for you." He reached into his pocket and took out a shiny hair clip. "Thought this'd look nice in your braids."

"Thank you," I replied, not making eye contact with him.

"Will you look at me?" He gently moved my chin so my face was facing his. No man other than blood family had ever touched me. His fingers felt coarse but gentle. My cheeks began to burn, and a strange sensation moved down my body as I looked into his eyes. I wanted to run my finger over his cheeks. I'd never seen skin that looked like a root-beer float made with chocolate ice cream—creamy froth just floating on the top that you'd want to lick up. I expected him to appear as old as my daddy, but he seemed more the age of my big brothers, maybe ten years older than I was. He had clear, honest, brown eyes and narrow cheeks that led to an almost pointed chin. His nose was wide and his lips full of promise just for me. He smiled as we looked at one another. "You're lovely, Nell. The prettiest girl for miles around. You have a special look, a look of someone who knows things."

"I read. That's how I know things. I always want to know more."

"I see you with books all the time. How'd you come to be such a reader?"

"Miss Parker taught me to read—not just to read but to

know people and places in books. She says a person can see the whole world by reading books. Do you read?"

"Not so much. Books weren't something we had at our home. I started working the farm when I could handle a shovel. Never went to school." He shrugged and threw a stone onto the path at the foot of the steps. "Would you like to live up North?" When he asked the question, he touched my back, tracing my spine with his fingertips. The tingling in my body got stronger, a strange but good feeling that made me press my legs tightly together.

"Why would I live there? My family's here."

Henry pulled out a handkerchief and wiped his forehead. It wasn't so hot that day. This was the time of year just after winter, before the harsh heat of the Louisiana sun burned through everything in its path. It was the best time of year to be outside, on the porch or in the fields or even in the kitchen; yet sweat rolled down his face, made a dark line on his collar and a wet stain beneath his armpits. He folded the handkerchief, placed it in his jacket pocket, took a deep breath, and said, "Nell, I'd like you to be my wife. We can start a family of our own up North. Another birthday gift for you."

I looked over my shoulder to see if Daddy was listening to us. No one was on the porch but Henry and me. I noticed Momma spying out the window, but she backed away when I saw her. "Well," I said. "I don't know you. I've watched you come here and sit with the men. Seems like you get along with everyone. I could be with you, but what about love? Don't married people love one another?"

Henry pulled me close to him; our bodies touched as he wrapped his arm around my shoulder. "Nell, I don't have much family left. I've been on my own for a time now. But I learned a lot from my parents. I watched them take care of one another, be kind and gentle. I think that's what love is, how it works." Then he kissed my cheek. I was torn between wanting to pull away from him and wanting more. I tugged at the hem of my cotton dress, smoothing it over my knees. That morning Momma had told me to put this particular dress on, the one I'd wear to church on Easter Sunday.

"I got family up North, in a place called Boston. It's a big city. I've been to visit, and I know I can make a good life there." Henry looked out at the road as he spoke, as if he were seeing something come alive in the dust. I could feel his longing and anticipation. It was the way I felt whenever I read my books. The place we sat was a good place, with family and the land to keep us alive, but I knew there was other air to breathe that wasn't full of hog smell and dry dirt that got caught in your throat all day long.

"It all sounds good, you know, getting married, moving away. I know that's what's supposed to happen. I'm grown now. It's just that—I think a girl should know the boy before she says *yes*. Don't you want to know me better too?"

He just stared at me. A look came across his face like a cloud blocking the sun. His features were suddenly obscure. Then a crease formed in the corner of his lips, not quite a smile but the possibility of a smile. "I do want to know you. I thought that would happen once we got married."

"Maybe we could do some knowing first." I looked directly into his eyes.

"So I guess this means you want to be *courted* before you'll give me an answer?"

Courted—I quickly searched my mind for this word, but I

couldn't find anyplace I'd ever seen it in a book or heard anyone use it. Courted—whatever it meant, it seemed to make
Henry slow down. So I said, "Yes, I'd like to be courted."

Henry massaged his forehead as if he were fighting off a
headache. "All right, Nell, I'll court you. Not what I was expecting, but I'll come by at the end of each day to visit."

"You'll be coming just to be with me, not with Daddy
and the other men?"

"Yes."

"And we can talk, maybe go for walks?"

"All right."

"And we can talk about books?"

"I don't read books, Nell."

"Then I can read to you. Would that be okay?"

"Yes, Nell."

I could feel my face shining bright, my smile so wide my
cheeks hurt.

"Well, I guess I best be going," he said, "It's getting
late." As he stood to leave he reached for my hand and gently kissed my palm. "I'll see you tomorrow, Nell." He turned
and slowly walked away, then stopped after a few steps and
turned to face me. "Nell, just so you know, I've been coming
here all this time because of you. Good night."

He had a little swagger in his step, as if he were dancing
on the balls of his feet. With each step he took, I imagined
me walking beside him, holding hands, listening to the birds,
each of us sharing our deepest thoughts. I imagined his lips
on mine, his hands exploring my body.

◯⊘

HENRY CAME TO the house every evening that spring to visit. When he arrived, he would greet my daddy first, then Momma; then he would nod to my brothers; and then he would ask for me. Momma told me, "Never be outside waiting for Henry. Always let him ask to see you. Let him watch you arrive." So I waited inside each evening, listening as Henry made pleasantries. When he'd shyly say, "Is Nell available to visit?" I'd glide in front of the screen door and stand there for a moment to make sure he could see me through the torn screen that never kept bugs or mosquitoes out. As soon as I pushed on the cracked wood frame, a loud squeak rose up from the rusted hinges—a trumpet announcing my arrival.

Henry's face lit up as he fussed with the cap dangling in front of him. "Hello, Nell. Fine evening to visit some, if you'd like to."

"Don't mind if I do."

We'd sit in a quiet corner of the porch away from Daddy, my brothers, and the other men. Momma would hurry inside after offering cool drinks. They could all see us but didn't pay much attention to our whispers and laughter or our touching and long, full, silences. If we were quiet for too long, though, sitting so close that air couldn't make its way between our arms or hips, the sound of Daddy's cough would prompt Henry to slide a few inches away from me. Every evening for two months our courtship unfolded that way. It was a new feeling to be with family on the porch, yet alone with Henry at the same time.

One evening Henry was fidgeting more than usual. When we sat down, he asked, "Nell, I hope you feel like you've gotten to know me over these months of courting. I have a good sense of who you are."

"Who do you think I am?"

"Well, you're smart, like to read, and know things. You're easy to be with. I like sitting with you and just talking. You feel good, your skin is soft, your hands are firm yet gentle. It's like you know how to work with your hands but take care of them too. I'm not sure you know your way around the kitchen, though. Your momma seems to be in control there."

"I know my way around books better than the kitchen. But I can learn."

"I'm sure you will—I suspect you can learn most anything."

"What else do you sense?"

"I think maybe you like me, the way I like you." He took my hand and opened my palm. He traced the dark lines on my hand, starting with the base of my thumb and moving up to the area just below my index and baby finger. I was fidgeting. He folded my fingers into my palm, making a soft fist with my hand, and asked, "What do you know about me now?"

"I know you're gentle. I like the way you touch me." He ran his finger over the top of my ear. "I like reading to you, I think you enjoy that. Do you?"

"Yes. Can't say I understand the stories, but I love your voice."

"Do you want me to explain the stories and the characters?"

"No. I can just listen."

"But don't you want to understand?"

"Not really, Nell. I'm more interested in stories of real life. I don't need make-believe people."

"Tell me one now, about your daddy."

He stopped touching me, folded his hands together, and looked down, playing with the front of his trousers where a crease should have been, picking up a small piece of dirt and flicking it away. "My daddy was a poor man—we're all poor in these parts, but my daddy was poorer than most. He didn't have a way with the land and animals like your daddy does. He'd work the soil, plant seeds, water them, but nothing ever grew. He'd get a hog or chicken, any kind of farm animal that could provide food for the table, and he'd feed it, but eventually it would just die off. He tried to teach me farming, thought maybe he was just jinxed and things would be different with me, but it wasn't so. You can't teach someone else to be good at what you can't do yourself."

I tried to imagine men-folk not being able to work the land, care for animals, put food on the family's table. I put my arm on Henry's and slid a little closer as he continued.

"Daddy decided he had to do something to keep our home. Momma was doing laundry for white women, cleaning their sheets, pillowcases, and tablecloths. She starched and pressed all day and night, earned enough to buy food, meager basics that she could make stretch for a long time. Daddy took to fixing things for other farmers. He was pretty good with a hammer and knew his way around motors and farm equipment. He taught me how to fix equipment. I'm good at it too. That's what I'll do up North—be a mechanic."

We sat in silence for a few moments. Henry seemed to be gathering his thoughts.

"I'm an only child. Momma couldn't get another baby to grow inside of her for some reason—only me. They were happy to have a son, but I always felt they missed the others."

"My teacher, Miss Parker, became an only child too. There aren't many families around here with just one child."

"Yes, Mary is alone, like me."

"Mary?"

"That's her name, your teacher, Mary Parker."

"You know her?"

"Everyone knows everyone in these parts." Henry went on, "One day Daddy was working on a large tractor. Something went wrong—the brake wasn't on or the tractor was at a bad angle. He was under it. It rolled over him. Crushed him. There wasn't anything anyone could do. I was supposed to be with him that day, but I didn't go—don't remember why—but I should've been there." Henry's voice had begun to crack. He squeezed my hand and said, "Nell, it's time for me to leave, make a place for myself in the North. Will you come with me, marry me?"

When Henry had agreed to court me, I hadn't known how long it'd be before he asked me to marry him again, or what answer I'd give. Now it felt right, and I thought the prospect of a new adventure was intriguing. "Yes," I said.

## Chapter Four

THE NEXT SUNDAY MY BEST DRESS WAS CLEANED, ironed, and hung out for me to wear. I'd been properly washed and powdered, my hair done in braids with ribbons and my shoes shined bright as Daddy's going-to-church pair. Momma made a veil using a plastic headband. She glued pretty flowing lace to the top, with enough hanging in front to cover my face. "I wore this lace when I married your daddy," she told me as she adjusted the veil on my head. "A girl needs something old to wear on her wedding day, and this lace is yours. My momma gave it to me. One day your daughter will wear it."

I only half heard her. Part of me was still laying in bed, savoring the first hours of the day when I'd had the morning to myself. I had awoken early. Daddy was getting ready to go out to the fields. Even though this was Sunday and my wedding day, there were things that needed doing on the farm. Daddy and Robert went about their chores. I lay in bed, listened to their movements, watched the thin rays of sunrise peek through the window. A solemn stillness overcame me. Morning always seemed like the hours of promise—when the quiet of night was letting go of darkness, just before the sounds of daily life consumed every corner of the house. This was the time to dream.

My mind wandered to thoughts of Henry as I stroked my skin beneath the quilt. Last night he had said my skin felt smooth. I imagined his fingers—slowly gliding down my arms, making circles on my stomach, touching my thighs, probing everywhere. Heat overcame me. I threw the quilt onto the floor and looked around the room, fearful that someone had seen me in such a state. I grabbed the book satchel from under the bed. Solace greeted me as I handled each book—my private family, who provided me with a direction different from what my blood family gave me. They would leave with me tomorrow, though I would take almost nothing else.

I held the books close to my chest and looked around my bedroom. Someone else would claim this as their room quicker than a grasshopper could jump from one spot to another. My quilt had been on this bed since I was old enough to sleep alone. It was a handmade creation, pieces of scrap fabric stitched together by Momma and other women. Momma told me that each piece of cloth had its own story. I loved the story about the pretty lace pieces that stood out against all the other prints, plaids, and rough potato-sack browns in the quilt. Momma told this story over and over. I could hear her voice as if she were in the room.

"My friend, Mrs. Sterling, worked for a white family, cleaning, washing, ironing, like most of us; but her important job was to keep the white woman's lace curtains and tablecloths bright and pressed. One day my friend asked to go home early. Her youngest had taken ill, and she wanted to be with her child. The missus was having a special tea for her friends the next day and told Mrs. Sterling no, there was too much that needed to be done. My friend pleaded with her, but the missus wasn't having anything to do with letting her go home to her family. Well, somehow all that pretty linen and lace ended up with mysterious brown spots on the edges, middle, everywhere you looked. The missus was so mad when she saw the mess, she took out some scissors and begun to scream and cut and tear her lace. She told Mrs. Sterling to get out of her house and never come back. My friend made like she had no idea what had happened. Maybe the water was bad...maybe it was the soap...maybe the iron needed to be cleaned. She begged the missus not to fire her, but it was done. Before she left the house, the missus told her to clean up the tattered lace and throw it out. Mrs. Sterling, with tears flowing down her cheeks, picked up all the lace, tied it into a bundle, and walked home with all of it.

"She brought the lace to our quilting session and told us the story, said she wanted to make a quilt with the lace and put some pieces of other fabric around it to finish it off. After a lot of discussion, we decided that the best way to use the missus's lace was for everyone to have a section, to spread her lace all over the county. That way her special lace would be on the beds of all the black children in these parts. And that's what we did." After she finished the story Momma would rub the piece of lace in the quilt, just as I was doing now. I wondered about having my own children and what stories I'd tell them.

Moving one leg, then the other, I slipped out of bed and began to tidy up. This would be the last time I made up this bed, folded and smoothed the quilt, fluffed the pillow, and tucked in the edges of the sheets. My hands began to shake ever so slightly. The corners of my eyes stung; my nose was running. Suddenly I couldn't move. It was like a scary night when I heard sounds outside. I'd want to get up and explore, but my body would stiffen while my mind raced, telling me at least to change positions.

After several deep breaths I took a few steps around the room. The old hand-made dresser, with five drawers and a mirror just big enough for me to see my face in the clouded glass, stood two paces from the bed. The things on the dresser included my little white bible, with gold-leaf edges on the pages and a gold cross etched on the cover. This was my baptismal gift. I had been dunked in the murky river on the Sunday after I completed my bible studies. The tiny wood box Daddy had carved for me held the only piece of jewelry I'd ever owned—Momma's earrings. She'd worn them on her wedding day—tarnished black metal with several diamond-like stones dangling from the ends. Once a day I'd screw the earrings on, flick the stones so they danced, and look at myself. Then, gingerly, I'd put them back in the box. A black comb missing several teeth, a wood-handled brush, and the hair clip Henry had given me. All my possessions were resting on the dresser. One picture, of Momma and Daddy, was tucked into the corner of the mirror. I'd take all of this with me.

Suddenly I began to feel like a ghost, as though I were floating above the room, looking down at everything, watching another soul move about the space and claim it as her own.

WE WENT TO church as a family, the way we did every Sunday, but on this day my wedding ceremony would take place before the regular service. Church was the one place where everyone throughout the county would gather to worship, socialize, and marry their daughters off to local boys. It was a tradition for weddings to take place on Sundays; that way the bride's family could count on the neighbors being present for the ceremony.

At the church I waited downstairs with Momma, Daddy, and Bernice, who was my matron of honor. Robert was Henry's best man. Henry hadn't counted on a formal wedding, so when I'd asked him which friend would be his best man, he'd had a blank look. But Robert had said he'd be proud to be part of my wedding.

Miss Parker came downstairs to pay a visit. "Nell," she said, "I have a gift for you." Out of her purse she took a gold chain with a small cross. "My daddy gave this to me when I was your age. I want you to have it. It has always brought me comfort." She put the necklace around my neck.

"Thank you, Miss Parker." I rolled the cross between my fingers.

"You look lovely, Nell. Such a pretty bride. I wish you all the best."

"Miss Parker, may I ask you something? I've learned so much from you, about books and all. And you've been kind enough to talk about your family. When I listened to you describe your momma and daddy, it sounded as if they were real happy together, like mine. What can you tell me about how to be happy with a husband? I mean, from what you grew up with in your home? Or are there some books I should read?"

"The best advice I can give is what my momma told me. She and Daddy always liked to dance around the kitchen or out on the porch. He'd take her by the waist and spin her around until she was dizzy, almost falling. Sometimes he'd reach for me and have us both spinning like plates on sticks. We'd laugh and clap until our bodies were tired and then collapse in a chair. I asked Momma once, why did they dance all the time? She told me, 'If you want to make your man happy and content, feed him good food and let him spin you around every now and then.' Best advice I have for you, Nell. My parents were happy right up until the time when the world wouldn't let them be."

"I like that advice."

"I never got to apply it myself, but I'm sure it'll work for you."

"Didn't you ever want to get married?"

"I almost did. But it wasn't meant to be. This is your day —enjoy it. Come back and visit. I'll want to know all about your life up North."

As Miss Parker walked out, a group of my girlfriends from school showed up. They pranced into the waiting room like a cloud of dust, bumping into each other and running to grab hold of me for hugs. Their voices rang out like one continuous bell singing in the air. "Nell, you look beautiful!" "How do you feel?" "Are you excited?" "Are you scared?" "Nervous?" "Henry's so cute!" "I hope to marry someone like him." "You sure are lucky." "Do you leave for up North right after the wedding?" "I can't imagine what it's like there. I hear it gets real cold." "Will you go to school there?" "What about babies?" "Babies? What about sex?" "Shush. Her momma can hear." "Are you ready for that?" "I'd be." "Sure. Like you know anything." "Do too." "No way!" "We'd better go, get our seats." "Congratulations, Nell. We're so happy for you." With one big group hug they hustled off, the same cloud of dust that had floated into the room moments earlier.

I got well wishes from my brothers and their wives, words of advice, and more hugs than I could count. I thought, "This is what a stuffed doll must feel like—tossed from one set of hands to another, with no one asking permission or waiting for a response." I kept smiling. My lips stuck to my teeth. My cheeks hurt. I wanted to be alone, find a quiet corner, curl up and read one of my books.

"Baby Girl, where are you?" Momma said. "You look as though you've drifted far away."

"I was just thinking, Momma."

"Let me fix your hair. Your friends managed to pull my beautiful braids loose."

I sat at the dressing table while Momma worked my hair again. She'd been doing it all day, and my scalp was beginning to hurt. I watched her in the mirror as her fingers twisted and folded my braids. The two fans in the room kept blowing strands of hair out of her reach, but she'd grab the rogue pieces and yank them back into place. At the same time, with the back of her hand, she managed to wipe sweat beads dripping from her forehead, never letting go of the braids.

"Momma, what do I need to know about being with a man?"

"You mean with a husband."

"Momma!"

"There's a difference."

"Well, I'm about to have a husband. What do I need to know? Ouch! That hurts!"

"Be still. Suppose I should've had this conversation with

you long before now. How does Henry make you feel? I mean inside your body."

"Real good. I can't stop thinking about him. Even before he says good night each evening, I start to miss him—I'm almost afraid I won't see him again. He holds me, and I want to guide his hand everywhere on my skin. When he kisses me, my body begs for more."

"Just listen to your body. It'll tell you what you need to know."

"But other times, Momma, it feels different."

"How?"

"It's as though . . . I'm not sure. If I'm with Henry for a while, sitting on the porch or walking, things go dark. Suddenly I can't see faces clearly—yours, Daddy's, the boys. Even the farm seems to disappear. I know it's still there, but shapes become less clear; all the sharp edges of our home and this town start to waver. Rather than holding closer to Henry, I pull away, fold into myself. Breathing becomes difficult, and my chest gets tight inside. It happened last Sunday, as we finished planning for the wedding and our move. He wanted to know what was wrong. I just shook my head, said I needed to get some rest. It felt good one moment. Then it was gone."

"I remember the day I was about to go to church and marry your daddy. I didn't have a lot of time to think about what was going to happen, the way you have, but still it was enough time to make my head swim and my stomach do somersaults. My parents were certain that Daddy was the right man for me. I wasn't in a position to say otherwise. And frankly, I don't think I knew one way or the other. I just did what I was told. But I do remember feeling like my world was about to change in ways I couldn't understand. I was leaving my family's home; moving into Daddy's with his family; saying good-bye to my momma and everything that mattered to me. I wasn't exactly happy, but I wasn't sad either. I think I was just confused and excited at the same time. Momma calmed me down by telling me how she and Daddy came to be married and happy, with a house full of children."

"Like you're doing now, with me?"

"Yes, Baby Girl. We find our way; women always do. There, braids are beautiful again."

"Think I'm ready, Momma?"

"Reckon you are."

DADDY AND I stood in front of the closed doors leading to the pews. One of the church ladies was facing us, her white-gloved hand on the door handle, poised to open it. I held tight to Daddy's arm, so firmly that he lifted my fingers to unlock my grip and then placed them back. He didn't look at me. I was staring at the closed doors as if seeing them for the first time. As often as I'd bounded through them, walked down the aisle to join my family in our pew for Sunday service, I had never noticed them before. They looked ancient, the dark wood scratched and dented at the bottom and around the handles. The hinges, probably polished brass at one time, were caked with rust. I wanted to take out a cloth and polish the tarnish away, to get lost in doing something that was my own to do, alone with my own thoughts.

My stomach tightened. I could feel bile rising up in my throat. Suddenly air seemed to evaporate from the hallway. My breathing became short and labored. I imagined I was underwater, watching bubbles rush to the surface. A faint glimmer of light pierced the water, reassuring me that life was up there, air was available if I could just get there in time. I was pushing up, up, up, praying my lungs wouldn't fail me, but they were burning, about to explode. Finally I broke through, tilted my head back, and hungrily drank in air while my body still flailed beneath the water.

"Baby Girl?" Daddy's voice brought me back to the hallway.

"Daddy. It's so far. Momma says I'm ready, but it's so far. I'm just sixteen!"

Daddy turned me to him. He held my shoulders with worry on his face and said, "You're my baby girl, always will be. But you're a woman now."

I tried to calm my breathing, swallow the bile, get my stomach to settle down. The shaking started in my kneecaps. I could almost hear them bouncing up and down. Then it traveled up my legs to my gut, like a terrible leg cramp trying to take control of my entire body. Sweat stains appeared under my armpits.

Daddy took out his handkerchief to wipe my forehead and nose. "You're gonna miss this heat," he said.

I took a deep breath. "Must be the heat getting to me."

"Tell me how you're feeling, Baby Girl."

"Daddy, I'm so jumbled up inside—scared but excited. It's like I'm facing my own yellow brick road. I want to step onto it, but I don't know what's up ahead. I'm excited about a life with Henry, but also afraid. He makes me feel like the whole world is there for us; all we have to do is be married and walk away. But what if I'm not happy away from home? What if I don't know what to do or how to act? With no family to help me, for me to turn to for comfort, what will I do when I'm in need? What if I can't make him happy, Daddy? What if it isn't like it's supposed to be when we're alone— you know—in bed? What if he regrets choosing me?

"And yet with all these questions, a part of me feels like I'm starving—I have a desperate need. You know the way you and the boys come in from the fields for lunch—you're so hungry. You attack the food that Momma and the women lay out on the table like it's the last time you'll get to eat. That's how this other side of me feels. I have an insatiable hunger, not so much for Henry, although that's some of it. I'm aching to know what my life could be. If I don't get it, I'll go mad. I know this doesn't make any sense, but that's what I'm feeling. Am I just crazy?"

"Not crazy, Baby Girl—just a young woman with a new man in her life and a taste for living. What would your characters tell you?"

"My characters?"

"In your books. What'd they say?"

"Well, I guess each would be different. Huck set out to explore new places and people, with a companion most thought he should not be with. Janie made her way through hot dusty towns of the South, trying to shape herself into the woman she was meant to be. Jo March, whose family had prepared her for a certain station in life, found she had to leave the safety of her family's home and create her own. And Alice, well, she took a path down the road and found friends and adventure along the way. She was scared, but it all worked out for her and the other characters, too. So maybe what they'd tell me wouldn't be so different."

"Listen to them, listen to your heart. You're one of the

strongest people I know. You'll always be our Baby Girl, and this will always be your home. We'll always be here for you." He kissed my forehead. "You ready?"

My lungs filled with air, so much so that my chest expanded, pushing my shoulders back, my chin reaching for the ceiling. "Reckon so." We turned towards the door. The usher nodded. Daddy looked at me and then motioned to her. She opened the doors. Every pew was full with family, friends, and neighbors. They all stood as the doors opened and the organist began playing. Garlands made from white ribbons draped the end of each pew. In the center of each garland was a cluster of magnolias. Their fragrance filled the air with a mix of strong floral and lemon zest that was fresh and sensuous. My eyes closed as the scent wafted over me. An image of our magnolia trees in full bloom, rows and rows as far as the eye could see, brought me back to a place of comfort, a place I would miss but that I hoped would always be within reach.

The aisle from the door to the pulpit looked miles long. So far away, I thought, so far. Looking left and right, I glimpsed smiles everywhere. Even if I couldn't make out exact faces, I was comforted by the warmth coming from them.

There in the distance was Henry. My heart jumped. The anxiety that had gripped my mind began to fade. Henry looked taller than ever. His suit and white shirt were crisp. He turned to face me. I wanted to let go of Daddy's arm, run into Henry's. It seemed as though my feet were no longer touching the floor. I was gliding down the aisle. We were suddenly the only people in the church. Our first night together was within sight. Henry would touch me everywhere. The scent of him would linger on my body for hours.

Then I remembered that I was in church and such thoughts weren't appropriate. But oh, how I wanted to taste him. Suddenly my cheeks flushed hot. My body was heaving again—now for a taste of Henry and a new life. I felt scared and excited, embarrassed and ashamed of my thoughts. Daddy must have sensed my confusion. He looked at me from the corner of his eye. A knowing smile crossed his lips.

Daddy and I joined Henry, Robert, and Bernice at the altar, facing the preacher. The preacher asked, "Who gives this woman, Nell Jones, to be wed to this man, Henry Bight?" Daddy said, "I give Baby Girl." He hugged and kissed me. Then he turned to join Momma.

But I stopped him, holding onto his arm. We both froze. His face got that worried look again as he searched my eyes. I could almost hear blood rushing to my forehead, pounding away, making me dizzy. I took a step toward Daddy, almost thinking that I'd rather join him in the pew with Momma than stay at the altar. My back was to Henry.

A sudden silence came over the congregation, a quiet lull of anticipation for what might happen next. Daddy loosened my grip on his arm. He put his hand on my cheek. I tilted my head into his palm, closed my eyes, and whispered, "Daddy." Neither of us moved for what seemed a long time.

At last Bernice said, "Nell, hand me your flowers."

As I turned to her, Daddy slipped away and joined Momma. Looking over my shoulder, I could see Daddy holding Momma as she wept. I turned back toward Bernice. She smiled and mouthed, "Okay?" I nodded my head, *yes,* took a deep breath, and turned to face the minister with Henry on my right.

He moved close to me and gently rubbed his shoulder

against my arm. That simple touch brought a smile to my face as brilliant as the sunlight streaming through the stained-glass window. My back was to Momma, Daddy, the boys, Miss Parker, my friends, and the people who had watched me grow up. But it was Henry's essence right next to me that filled my heart with calm. At that moment I thought I might actually be able to love him.

MOMMA WAS IN the kitchen, her hands deep in sudsy sink water, cleaning dishes from the celebration feast. I could see shadows streaming in from the window, dancing across her back as she rhythmically swayed from side to side. Streams of sunlight bounced around the kitchen, highlighting the dust that lingered on surfaces and in corners. Tiny particles floated in the streams, seemingly moving in rhythm with Momma. The shadows played games with my eyes. For a moment she no longer resembled my momma but someone else, a younger version of herself, an older promise of me.

"Baby Girl, why you watching me?" She kept her back to me as she spoke.

"How'd you know I am?"

"I can feel your eyes through the back of my head." She turned to look at me.

"I'm married now, Momma," I sighed, looked around the room as though I were seeing everything in the kitchen for the first time. The spice canisters, older than I was, shimmered in the sunlight, the dark spots and dents in the pots resting on the stovetop disappeared in the light. *Married.* I repeated the word under my breath, gazing around the room that held so many smells and sounds. I wanted to imprint them all in my mind. The floor—faded, the corners of the black and white linoleum curling—almost looked smooth and even, as it must have years ago.

"Come, sit." She pulled two chairs up. We sat with our knees touching, but mine kept bouncing up and down, as if I were dancing in place on the balls of my feet. Momma gently pushed on my knees to hold them down. She took my hands and pressed one on each knee. Then she held my cheeks between her hands, tilted my face toward her, and kissed my forehead.

The first tear dripped down the side of my face. My whole body began to shake. I leaned over, buried myself in Momma's lap, and grabbed her waist. She stroked my back and said, "My baby. No need to be scared." My chest was heaving so badly I couldn't catch any breath in my lungs. My shoulders kept pumping up and down as tears streamed from my face onto her dress.

Momma took her apron and wiped my face. She pulled a hankie from her pocket. "Blow your nose and settle down. We're gonna talk for a bit, and I need you to hear me."

"Yes, Momma," I mumbled, between sobs that sounded like a bad case of hiccups.

"I wasn't much older than you when I married your daddy. Can't say that I've done what I always wanted to do, and I can't tell you what to do with your life. You're different from me, different from your sisters, and that's all right. It's going to cause you trouble, already has, but you a strong person. For me strength is in being with your daddy, like my momma told me to. I never questioned anything, I did as I was told—that's the way it was when I was your age, and still that way for me." Absently she rubbed my cheeks.

It was as if she were feeling not my face but her own from long ago.

"Didn't you want to marry Daddy?"

"There you go again, asking what no child has a business asking!" She pulled her hands away and sat straight up in the kitchen chair.

"I'm sorry."

"I love your daddy. Think I always did, even when I didn't know it at first. My momma and daddy brought him home one day, told me this would be my husband. Never asked me if I wanted to get to know him, and I certainly didn't tell him he had to *court* me before I'd give an answer. I just knew the marriage was gonna be. Maybe somewhere, way back in my mind, there was a whisper, a sense that I should have a say in who I married, but the voice, that feeling, was so faint, it faded away like morning dew once the sun makes its presence known." Her gaze wandered off, somewhere above my head.

"You and Daddy look perfect together. Like you were meant for each other."

"Oh, we're perfect all right—perfect in our imperfections. You'll find that kind of perfect with Henry too."

"Momma. I need to ask you something. It's about Miss Parker. Do she and Henry know each other?"

Momma curled her face up with a quizzical look. "Everyone knows each other around these parts."

"That's what Henry said when I asked him."

"Why you asking, Baby Girl?"

"I don't know. It's just a feeling. Seems there's more to their knowing each other than this being a small place." I fiddled with the cross hanging from my neck.

"You know Henry is older than you—twenty-six. A man that age has had other experiences, maybe even other women. Doesn't mean anything. Now he's your husband, you his wife. Anything that came before—doesn't matter. That's all you need to know, and don't go asking him any more questions about who he knew in the past. Even if the question starts to rumble in your belly, travel up your throat, begin to foam in your mouth like a sick day—you push it back down. Just swallow it. No matter how bad it tastes, you don't let it out. Some questions a wife never puts out into the world—they'll just get mess all over you and everyone around. You understand?"

"Yes, Momma."

But I knew I wasn't like Momma. A bad taste has to get out sometime.

We sat in silence for a few moments. The knot in my stomach, which had eased a bit, grew hard again, as if someone had curled my insides into a fist and was twisting away.

Then Momma said, "I'm gonna miss you, Baby Girl. Here, I want you to take something with you." She handed me the quilt from my bed. It was folded as tight as could be into a large square, with string tied into a bow holding the colorful fabric in place. A piece of the white lace was positioned beneath the bow. "You take this with you and rest it on top of your children, my grandbabies-to-be. That way you'll always have something to hold that was just yours, all your life, and you can tell your little ones the story about this fine lace."

My body caved. I fell into her lap, digging my fingers into her apron, while she soothed my pain with humming, running her hands up and down my back.

"What's going on with my women folk? You fixin' to spend the afternoon in here?" Daddy said as he walked into the kitchen. But when he saw the state I was in, he joined Momma in rubbing my back. "Baby Girl," he said, "you remember how I taught you to hold a knife and slice an apple?" I could barely hear his voice over my sobs. I shook my head.

"You had to hold the knife at just the right angle or you'd prick yourself, draw blood. Remember? And the apple, you had to cradle it in the palm of your hand and be gentle with it as you sliced the peel and then took small pieces to eat."

"Yes," I said between sniffles, beginning to straighten up.

"Well, think of the apple as your marriage to Henry. You need to hold it gently. And the knife—well, a knife can do good or it can do harm. You have to decide which, whenever it's in your hand."

I studied their faces the way a doctor might examine a patient, to understand what each mark, mole, indentation, piece of hair meant. Daddy's dark brown eyes had red veins traveling in what must have been clean white circles at one time—years ago, before all his hard work and labor bent him like the branches of an aged tree. Momma's face had craters from bearing and raising babies, cooking and cleaning. In her eyes was a wistful look, the ghost of forgotten dreams. I saw the shadows of them and of my life here, as sunlight waned in the kitchen and the dancing dust particles disappeared.

## Chapter Five

WE RODE FOR DAYS FROM ONE SMALL TOWN TO another, in crowded buses filled with people the likes of which I'd never seen. There were children hanging onto their mommas' dresses. They weren't so different from the young ones I was accustomed to seeing at the farm, in town, or at school, except these children had different shades of color to their skin. Some were as black as my family and me—on our skin charcoal marks would go unnoticed—but others were the color of the fields and wild grasses after months of winter—golden, almost lustrous, as though the sun were shining on their foreheads. I thought one family was white, but if they'd been white they wouldn't have been in our section of the bus—way in the back, crowded together even though there were empty seats in front.

Henry read my quizzical look. "We come in lots of colors, you'll see," he said. "But remember—black is black, no matter how pale the shade."

We didn't speak much during our journey, but he was kind and gentle with me. The buses were our transportation and lodging. Whenever the driver told us we'd be at a certain stop for a few hours until the next bus arrived, we found a place to get some food. If I looked cold, Henry would put his arm around me. If I looked sleepy, he would gingerly move my head to rest on his shoulder. He would explain where we were, the variations between small and large Southern towns, the differences between the rural South and the industry of the North.

Once we had passed through Georgia the roads kicked up less dust; hard surfaces were everywhere. Buildings looked taller, stood closer together, and the people getting on and off the buses changed as well. There were still many like me—farm people with the smell of animals permanently imbued in our clothes. Others, though, had newness about them, freshness, like Miss Parker. I guessed their shoes didn't spend time in slop or mud, and their hands weren't thick from working in the fields. They carried books, magazines, and newspapers.

There must have been some magical line we crossed between South and North. I didn't see anything in particular announcing the change except for the public bathrooms. I was exhausted and excited when we arrived at the Boston bus station. "This is our new home, Nell. You're going to like it here, I promise," Henry reassured me, as he watched me gazing at the activity in the bus station—people everywhere, shoving and bumping into one another; vendor stands with candy, magazines, newspapers; a loud voice booming in the air, announcing the comings and goings of buses. I almost fell from turning in circles, trying to take it all in.

"Where're the animals?" I asked.

"You won't see animals here, not like back on the farm. Here you'll see people, buildings, stores, cars, buses—the things a big city has to offer."

My spinning overcame me; suddenly my insides felt squeamish. "I have to pee."

"Ladies' room over there." Henry pointed to the farthest

door on the right. He then started walking toward the door marked *Men.*

I walked past the door marked *Ladies,* looking for my door, the door marked *Colored.*

"Nell, where're you going?" Henry said.

Just then a woman who had been sitting behind us on the bus came up to me. "This your first time? Mine too. We'll go in together."

She and I inched our way to the ladies' room door and peeked inside. There was a white woman at one of the sinks. She looked up at us but then went about washing and drying her hands without giving us any mind. When she was finished, she came toward us, said *excuse me,* and walked right past us. We watched her walk away; then we stepped into the bathroom. It looked like other bathrooms we'd seen, the ones marked *Colored:* a row of white porcelain sinks with mirrors and soap; paper-towel containers on the walls over the trash cans; four toilet stalls. Everything was clean, even the smell, as if the place had just been scrubbed down. The woman and I each chose a stall and did our business. I went to the sink to wash my hands and noticed that a line had formed outside, filled with both white and colored women. I was scared to see all of them standing waiting for me to finish. I watched a white girl walk over to my stall—she didn't even hesitate, just went right in after me. As I headed to the door, I looked at the other people and said *excuse me* to a white woman. She smiled at me and stepped aside.

My companion and I went out into the station together. "Henry!" I shouted. "We used the same washroom as everyone else. The same stalls, sinks, towels! Everything! I've never seen anything like it."

Henry nodded. "I told you, Nell, it's different in the North. You won't see *White* or *Colored* signs around here." Pointing at the water fountain he said, "Look, there's the water. No signs over that either. Anyone can walk right over and get a sip from the same spigot. That's how it is, Nell. That's why I want to make our home here."

"So much for me to learn; school will help."

"No school—you won't have time for that. You'll be too busy putting our home together, taking care of us, and having babies. I'll teach you all you need to know."

"I know we'll have a family, but there's time for that, we don't have to rush. What about books? I'll always want to read."

"There's a building full of books here—it's called a library. You can find all the books ever written right there and take them home to read. Then you return them for someone else. It's like a borrowing system. Best of all, it's free. I'll teach you how to use the library."

"Henry, when do the babies start?" For days Henry and I had sat tightly next to one another on buses, and only now, standing in the hectic Boston bus station, were we having a personal conversation. "When?" I asked again.

Henry was busy cleaning his shoes. With one foot raised on top of a bench, he rubbed the dust and dirt from the leather shoes, buffed them as best he could, trying to get a spit shine on the tips. He seemed to lose himself in the shoes. "A man should always have clean, polished shoes. My daddy told me that. No matter if you live on a farm. When a man goes out in the world, his shoes need to look professional; they tell a story about how he respects himself."

I waited for him to notice me. "When, Henry?"

Finished with his shoes, he said, "When we get home."

"But, Henry, we don't need to have a baby right away. There's so much for me to learn and explore. I'll want to set up house, walk around the neighborhood, meet neighbors, find out where to get food and supplies. I'll need to be comfortable in this new world before I can handle a baby."

"Nell, a man and a woman make a family. That's how it's meant to be. You know this from back home. Women folk have babies and take care of their families. That's what you'll do here."

"I want to wait!" The words bolted out of my mouth quick as lightning dancing against a dark night sky.

Henry glared at me and crossed his arms. His lips were pressed tight. His jaw moved as if he were chewing on something. He looked down at his shoes, over my head, then at me. "Tell you what. We can start having sex right away, but that doesn't mean we'll have a baby. We can decide when to actually make a baby."

"How? I thought sex and babies went together."

"It does, but it's possible for a couple to plan when they want to make a baby. In the weeks between your monthly, if we have sex then, you can't get pregnant."

"My monthly just finished—that's why I felt sick on the bus. I always get a sour stomach each month. Sometimes the cramps are so bad it feels like my insides are being attacked and kicked around. Momma said that means my body is fertile."

"See, that's good. I mean about it just ending. So when we get home, sex'll be okay; no worry about a baby. And it's good Momma said your body is fertile."

"Why's that good?"

"When we decide to start making babies, your body'll be able to make as many sons as I want."

"And girls."

"Of course, girls too, for you."

I looked around at the women in the bus terminal. There were several pushing baby carriages or holding infants in their arms. A few women with swollen bellies were struggling to walk and carry suitcases. White or colored, they were all dressed better than I was; I still looked like a farm girl, with old shoes on my feet, hair sticking out all over, wrinkled clothes. Yet the look on their faces made me shudder; they reminded me of all the women back home. There was no shine to their eyes, although it was difficult to see clearly into eyes downcast, with heavy lids. Daddy's old mule had the same look, its body curved and bent from carrying too much weight, expected to continue on when all it wanted to do was stop and be left alone.

"Ready to go home, Nell? I'm eager to settle down with you."

"Henry, are you sure, about babies, that we can plan when? All these women, they have the same tired look as all the women back home. It's as though they're carrying a heavy burden that slows them down. I'm not ready for that Henry, may never be. We need to build our marriage, need time for ourselves for a while."

"Of course I'm sure. Come here—you ready for this?" He pulled me to him and kissed me hard. His tongue thrust into my mouth. I pressed my body against his and wrapped my arms around him. Then suddenly he pushed me away. "Let's go, we have some loving to do."

# *Chapter Six*

*HOME* TURNED OUT TO BE A COLD-WATER FLAT ON the fourth floor of a six-story brick apartment building. The idea of a cold-water flat didn't have much meaning for me then. On the farm all of our water was cold, brought into the house from the well outside. Hot water was made by boiling it in cast-iron pots on the stove. Usually on bath days we'd take a bucket of fresh, cold water and wash ourselves with a cloth—*bird bath*, Momma called it.

The one room of the flat, which served as our bedroom, living room, and kitchen, wasn't large, but it wasn't too small either. The best thing was the bathroom, separate, with plumbing. No more outhouses for me; no more holding my water at night praying I wouldn't wet the bed; no more checking the corners of the smelly latrine for snakes, hornets, or spiders lurking in the shadows. I got to pee inside, got to flush the toilet and watch the mess disappear. The North was proving to be a good place.

Henry was true to his word when he told me that sex would start once we got home. That first night, I was scared. We had never been alone in all the months of courting; someone was always in earshot of us. Henry held me tight, kissed me hard on the lips the way he'd done at the bus station, then said, "Time to get undressed, Nell." I stood still, looked down at the floor. "Here, I'll help you." He unbuttoned the front of my dress to my waist, slipped the sleeves off my shoulders. I let my arms come out of the cloth as he pulled the dress down over my hips, so it lay in a puddle on the floor at my feet. I studied the folds of cloth around my ankles, the tips of my shoes peeking out like mice hiding under steps.

"Take off your underthings. Let me see you." He stepped back to watch. I pushed the dress aside on the floor, untied the laces and stepped out of my shoes, then moved them alongside the crumpled dress. The cracked wood floorboards felt coarse under my bare feet. I lifted the slip over my head and slowly removed the rest of my underclothes. Then I wrapped my arms across my chest.

Henry began to touch me. He ran his hands over every inch my body, turned me around so he could see my front, back, and sides. I pulled away as he started to touch my private parts, but he gently brought me closer to him and said, "I'm your husband, you my wife. All this is mine." Then he undressed. He guided my hands on his body. When he reached for his privates he said, "This is yours. Just relax, I'll teach you everything."

At one point that night, it felt as though I were floating in clouds. Our bodies became rhythmic, moving in sync as though we were two instruments playing in harmony after years of practice and rehearsals. We formed one mass on the bedsheets that were twisted and damp from our heat. Henry whispered suggestions in my ear about how to touch him, how to move, what positions to take; I did whatever he said. My body was in a frenzy to get more of him.

I didn't know how much time had passed that night before we were both so spent that we fell into a deep sleep, tightly wrapped in each other's arms. When I did awake, it scared me to see blood on my legs and the sheets. I shook Henry. "Something's wrong with me."

"Blood the first time is a good thing," he said. "Now I know I have a pure wife."

The next morning we had sex again—didn't bother to change the sheets, just kept pulling at one another, rolling and vibrating in the bed. I started to get comfortable with the things Henry told me to do. My body felt good when I relaxed into his rhythm.

I was awakened the second night with him on top of me, moaning, moving inside me. When he was done, he rolled off and went back to sleep. It wasn't so bad. At least I didn't have to guess about what to do.

However, on our third day in Boston and in bed, I began to feel real hungry and musty, the way my brothers used to be when they came in from the early-morning fields, ready for a hearty breakfast. "Henry, we need more to eat than snacks, and we should get cleaned up." I slid out of bed and headed to the bathroom, thinking that it would be fun to take a bath—the first time indoors, with running water to soothe my sore and tired body.

"I'll get some hot food and groceries, be right back." He jumped out of bed, pulled his trousers and shirt on, and headed to the door.

"Wait," I said. "I want to go too."

"No—you take a bath, be all cleaned up, ready to eat and ready for more of me." He kissed me and left. For a moment I wanted to protest and follow him out the door, but the prospect of being in the bathtub called out to me like the aroma of Momma's warm breakfast biscuits wafting into my bedroom each morning.

I sank into the bath water all the way up to my chin and closed my eyes. Every inch of my body tingled from the hot, steamy water and from the lingering sensations of our love-making. During our few days together, sensitive spots on my body that I had never known existed began to speak to me, saying—more! A warm glow emanated from my pores even before the hot water brought a red hue to my skin.

When Henry came home I was sitting on the side of the bed, wrapped in a towel. In one hand he held a bag with hot food that smelled like fried chicken and mashed potatoes, which he placed on the tiny stove. Then he put a brown grocery bag on the lopsided wooden kitchen table. In it were greens, corn, milk, eggs, and ground beef. "Come here." He took my towel, dropped it to the floor. "You look real pretty. I missed you." His lips pressed against mine, the weight of his body forced me onto the table. My hunger for food began to fade as our movements knocked the groceries onto the floor. For a brief moment a stream of sunlight peeked through the window, casting brightness into the room. Then a dark cloud appeared, and a smattering rain kissed the glass like sorrowful teardrops.

I CLUNG TO Henry's guidance as tightly as I held onto the words in my books. We walked the aisles of the local markets where chickens were already dead—feathers plucked, bodies washed, heads off, ready for seasoning and cooking. We picked out onions, peas, carrots, lettuce—all clean and some in packages. The rice came in boxes and cornmeal in cardboard containers, not in burlap sacks as they had at the general store. He showed me how to choose each item, looking for just the right freshness, color, and feel. I already knew how to cook—one of the many things I learned in Momma's kitchen—but Henry had some favorite dishes that I had to cook just right. He was particular about his meatloaf and showed me how his momma had made the dish. He wrote it all down for me, but I didn't mind; it was easier knowing that he was getting what he wanted, so I didn't have to guess about things.

Henry took me to the library one day, while we were taking a stroll through the neighborhood. It was an enormous building, with rows of concrete steps leading up to tall pillars flanking brass-looking doors with long handles that you had to pull hard to open. Inside, it was quiet and peaceful. I lost my breath when I looked up and saw the stacks and stacks of books, neatly arranged on shelves reaching from the first floor all the way up to the high ceiling.

Henry smiled when he saw the look on my face. "What do you think, Nell?"

For a moment I couldn't speak. "It's beautiful."

"Books really mean this much to you?"

"They do. I bet Miss Parker knows all about places like this, but this is mine. Can I read here, at these tables? Can I touch the books? How many do you think are here?"

"Lots."

"I'll want to read as many books as possible. When you're at work, I'll come here, choose a book, sit, and read. Right there, in that sunny window. That'll be my spot." I imagined I would spend many afternoons here while Henry was at work. This is where I'd learn about the world, find relief from our tiny apartment, discover instant companions in the characters whose lives and voices I'd come to know. This would be my sanctuary.

"I'll bring you here so you can take books home to read. It's better for you to read at home."

"Why? This is a wonderful place. I'm alone at home. At least here I'll see people, maybe strike up a conversation or two."

"I want you home when I'm at work. That's where you belong."

"Can I take some books now?"

"You need a card for borrowing."

"Let's get the card."

He hesitated for a moment, then filled out the paperwork.

"Here," said the lady behind the desk as she handed me the card. "Show this whenever you want to check out a book."

Henry grabbed the card before I could touch it.

I asked her, "Where can I find books like *Their Eyes Were Watching God* or *Little Women*?"

"In literature. Everything is listed by author." She pointed to the section of the room near the sunny window I'd admired.

"Henry," I said, "I'm going to find a book or two to take home."

"I'll walk with you."

"Please! Let me walk alone, I want to feel this space."

"Okay, but I'll be right in that chair. Stay where I can see you."

The aroma of the library washed over me. It was as though I'd opened my satchel and sniffed the collection of books permanently residing inside. I ran my fingers over the spines of different volumes, turned my head sideways to read titles and author names, noticed that some had shiny jacket covers while others were older, with frayed edges suggesting that many hands had caressed the stories inside.

When I reached the end of the aisle, I turned to see if Henry was watching me. He had slumped down in the leather chair, his arms resting on his chest. His legs were stretched straight out and crossed at the ankles. I could see that his eyes were closed; his chin moved up and down from easy breathing. I slipped around the corner, out of sight.

The next aisle was as full as the first, with books of different shapes, sizes, and colors lined up in perfect order. I decided to take a book with very frayed edges; I thought it must be one of the best, since it was so well worn. Along the window wall were small desks, one behind the other. Young people were using several of the desks, surrounded by books —they were probably students doing research of some kind. I took a seat at the only available desk and immediately felt like a student again. The wood had been etched with initials and heart signs, just like our little wood desks in Miss Parker's classroom. We had never been allowed to mark the desks, but somehow the signs of youthful love managed to appear, just as they had here. A warm ray of sunlight crossed over the desk, my face, and the open pages of the book. I closed my eyes and let the cozy corner fill me with hope.

"Nell, I told you to stay where I could see you."

Henry's voice startled me out of my reverie. I jumped up, knocking the chair to the floor as the book slammed shut.

Everyone looked up from their books and stared at us. "Sorry. I got caught up in the books."

"Did you find what you want?"

"Yes."

"Then let's go."

I picked up the book. As we sped down the aisle to the counter, I grabbed another one with a shiny cover. The lady asked for the library card. I turned to Henry, hopeful that he'd hand the card to me and that I in turn could give it to her. But he ignored my open hand as if it didn't exist and gave the lady my card.

She stamped the due-date cards for each book and slipped them into the sleeves on the inside back covers. Then she purposefully handed the books to me and said, "Enjoy." I saw her place my library card inside the sleeve with the due-date card.

"Thank you." I said.

# Chapter Seven

IN JUNE I REALIZED THAT I HADN'T HAD CRAMPS SINCE the bus ride, nor seen any red stains or had to rush to the toilet with a sick stomach. I liked the way my body felt because of our lovemaking. My scalp was tender to the touch, my ears tingled with the slightest head movement. I didn't want to remember that frightful monthly pain that could force me into a fetal position for hours. Momma had told me I had the same monthly problems she had as a young girl; over time the pain would let up, once the babies started to come. I didn't want a baby yet, and Henry had assured me that we could plan when the baby would come, no matter how often we had sex. But there hadn't been stains in my panties since the first night we made love, in April.

"We need to see a doctor," Henry announced, after I told him I'd missed my monthly. "I'll ask around at church or work, find a good one."

"I thought we'd be able to plan. This is too soon." My head was spinning with the possibility of having a baby right away.

"A family is just what we need."

"I'm not ready, Henry."

"I am."

⌒⑥

MONTHS LATER, I studied myself in the bathroom mirror while Henry finished breakfast. My body had taken on strange proportions with pregnancy. The little bit of sausage and eggs I'd nibbled had already found the inside of the toilet bowl. Our apartment was small, but today the walls seemed to close in, making it impossible to breathe. I'd lost sight of my ankles in the swollen mass my body had become.

When I joined Henry at the table, he didn't look at me but rubbed my stomach as though it were his own; placing his ear against me to discern sounds of his baby moving inside, he said, "He's growing pretty fast." His facial stubble scratched the tender skin of my belly. I winced but didn't pull away. "Gotta go" were his only words to me as he sped out the door.

I spent the morning cleaning the breakfast dishes and making the lumpy bed. The old mattress held onto the indentations of our bodies like molded dough; my quilt fit at the foot of the bed as decoration. As I folded and smoothed it flat, the colorful patches of fabric, hand-sewn stitches, and white lace pieces felt heavenly against my fingers. I could see the faces of Momma and the other ladies, hear their voices as they sat on the porch, chatting and quilting away. One would tell a story about her missus, the others would chime in with their version of the same story. Momma would shush them, reminding everyone that we children were within earshot. "Some things children shouldn't know about too soon," she'd admonish them. But we heard and hung onto every word they shared about their lives working in white folks' homes. These memories brought welcome comfort to the cold silence in my new home.

Once the uneven wood floor was swept, the bathroom sparkling clean, the dresser dusted, and my little box arranged in its rightful spot, I grabbed a book and sat by the only window blessed with a minuscule stream of sunlight to read. I had the books from my satchel and the books Henry borrowed from the library. I told him the type of story I wanted to read—about young people making their way through life, encountering adventure, overcoming obstacles, always learning and growing. I'd hoped he'd be able to convey this to the people at the library, so that they could tell him which books to borrow. Whatever he brought home I read. Some of the stories were good, others not, but I read them just the same. One day I asked him to bring home some newspapers, figuring there might be things going on in the neighborhood or the world that I could read about. He told me, "No, old books are enough to keep you company."

I wrote letters home, just as I had promised my parents. It was odd writing the first letter. I didn't know how to start it. Miss Parker had taught us what the salutation was supposed to be. Sometimes she had us write letters to each other in class, and I would write, "Dear Barbara" or "Dear Tom." But how was I supposed to address my parents? I tried "Dear Mother and Father," but that sounded formal, not like me at all. "Dear Momma and Daddy" sounded young, as if I were still a little girl sitting on the front steps, hair twisted in knots, random pieces of straw caught between my braids —not a married woman and soon-to-be mother. Finally I landed on "Dear Mom and Dad."

In my first letter I wrote about our long bus ride to Boston, the glimpses I had of the countryside and then of the cities as we traveled south to north. It reminded me of our walks down the dusty roads from the farm to the city nearby; yet this was bigger, vaster. I stretched out the little I'd seen to form a blanket around a city I had yet to see. And in this way, too, I made my small walk from our flat to the library sound like an adventure. I spoke of the children playing in the fire-hydrant springs, the way they reminded me of the river back at home. I described the thick green leaves that blossomed on the oak trees, mentioning how much I missed the beauty and scent of our magnolias. I explained that hearing neighbors' sounds had become part of the rhythm of our home—feet stomping overhead while loud music was playing, doors opening and slamming shut with children running in and out, the hallway filled with a cacophony of smells from different foods being cooked in each apartment.

It was easy not to share that I had seen the streets only a few times so far, and never alone, only with Henry; that mostly I sat in a chair by the window, looking out at the world through old curtains and cracked dirty glass, leaning on the chipped sill. I wanted to write about the red blotches that had mysteriously appeared on my face this morning, making me look as if a case of child measles were consuming me, about the insatiable urges that had suddenly overcome me last night, for food I didn't even care for, about how I could be cold one moment and hotter than a hog in heat the next, with sweat pouring from my skin. I wanted to ask Momma what I should do to prepare for childbirth, how would I handle the pain, what it would be like to mother with no mother nearby to guide me. I didn't dare speak about the unending hunger Henry had for my body, and the relief I had gained only now, with another life growing inside. I wanted to ask why it felt as if I must give up my dreams so that Henry could have whatever he wanted.

I knew my letters were for everyone—Daddy, the boys, their wives, and even family friends; they'd all get to hear about my adventure up North. So I wrote about the beauty of the tall, brick row-houses with steep steps leading up to painted wood doors, the black window boxes filled with colorful spring flowers, perfumed bouquets inviting elegantly dressed people strolling by to pause and enjoy the scent. I couldn't write about my deferred dreams.

Miss Parker had introduced us to Langston Hughes's poem "A Dream Deferred." Its meaning had been obscure to us, even after she explained the impact of slavery and oppression on a person's soul. But I remembered liking the sound of the words, the way Miss Parker had recited the poem without reading from the page, her eyes closed, and the long silence once she was finished. As children we had failed to grasp the import of the poem in our own lives. Sitting here now, alone, anxious to become the woman I thought I would be, the poem's meaning began to rub against my heart and drift in and out of my consciousness, like an echo bouncing off the walls of a great empty hall.

Sleep overcame me. It was then that my dreams could come alive.

*The woman walked down the street wearing a freshly pressed dress, nice shoes, a purse dangling from the crease of her elbow, a stylish hat on her head, with her finely coiffed hair peeking out on her forehead and over her ears. She stopped to chat with the neighbors across the street, to*

*say hello to the shopkeeper from whom she always pur-*
*chased newspapers and writing materials. She patted the*
*young child, who was bent over playing with marbles, and*
*waved to a friend passing in a car, someone who would oc-*
*casionally stop in for a cup of tea. This woman was on her*
*way to the library. Once there she would find her place in*
*front of the circle of small chairs where the children sat and*
*begin to read. It was her job to spend several afternoons a*
*week reading to youngsters from the story books in the chil-*
*dren's section. The children would sit quietly, giving her the*
*same attention she had always given to her teacher. After*
*answering the children's questions, congratulating them on*
*the few words she asked them to read, saying good-bye, and*
*tidying up, she would sit by herself, in the sunniest spot in*
*the library, reading the book she had chosen for the day.*
*Hours passed, and the sun grew warm on her face, tickling*
*the hairs on her arms. There was something hidden behind*
*her visage of happiness.*

The scratch of metal against metal as the key turned in
the lock, the sound of footsteps entering the room, Henry's
voice bellowing, "Nell!"—all these shattered my dream into
tiny pieces that tumbled to the floor like so many shards of
broken glass. "What's wrong?"

"Nothing. Guess I fell asleep."

"Where's dinner?"

"I haven't started yet."

"My baby okay?"

"Yes, baby's fine. I just..."

"You just what?"

"Henry, I'm tired and bored. I need something else.
More than just cooking, cleaning, sitting here waiting for

you to come home. This isn't what I thought life would be."

"*More*, like what? This here's your home. Taking care of it and me, preparing for my baby, this is what you're supposed to do; this *is* life."

"Look at me, Henry. A scarf's tied around my head; my fingers are thick like ankles; I can't work my hair, can't make braids like Momma used to. It's hot in this tiny apartment; I sit by the window hoping for a little breeze to cool the sweat on my brow, under my armpits. My ankles have become tree trunks; I can barely get shoes on, my feet so swollen. I've run out of paper to write letters; I've read all the books you've brought home. I need more. I want to go to the library again, visit the store, walk out this door, meet and talk to people, feel cool air on my face."

He turned his back to me, walked to the closet, and pulled out his shoe-cleaning materials. First he spread the oil cloth on the floor at the foot of the bed; then he took the can of black polish and gingerly placed it on the cloth. Beside the can went strips of an old undershirt he would use to apply the polish, then a short-haired brush with a dark wood handle. After removing his shoes, he began to rub the polish in slow circular motions on the tips, sides, and backs. Without looking at me, he said, "You bored, there are some men at the shop with no woman in their lives. They'd appreciate having clean, pressed shirts too. I can bring some home for you to do."

"No!" I braced my hands on the chair and pushed my body up, leading with the baby bump. I stumbled for a moment, then finally stood as straight as I could and faced him. "I will not clean other men's shirts!"

"No need to get riled up. You said you're bored—I

thought this would be a way for you to keep busy, that's all. No need to fight about it."

"Henry . . ." A stabbing jolt of pain in my stomach cut my voice off, and I let out a loud, "Ouch!" The room began to spin. It felt as though I were moving in slow motion. The floor came closer and closer to my face.

Henry gasped, "My baby!" He put his hands under my armpits, stopped my fall, then guided me to the bed. "Lay back." Gently he stroked my stomach, the same way he'd been rubbing his shoes, fluffed the pillow under my head, pulled the quilt over me. "Didn't mean to upset you. Look, this weekend I'll take you to the library, and the store to get paper. There's a beauty shop not far; we'll go there, let someone else do your hair like Momma did. Forget what I said about other men's shirts. You're fragile—with my baby and all."

The scent of shoe polish was something I had enjoyed when we first moved to Boston. It was almost luxurious— the oil-filled aroma that wafted into the air as Henry twisted the little hook on the side of the black can, allowing the fragrance to escape. Now, however, I felt more nauseated from the heavy odor of the polish on his fingertips as he stroked my belly than I did from the constant gurgling in my stomach. I rolled onto my side, held tight to the quilt, and tried to make the bed stop whirling beneath me.

SATURDAY MORNING I skipped around the apartment, prepared breakfast, bathed, and put on the best dress I had for walking outside. Henry on the other hand, dragged himself out of bed as though a heavy weight were pressing against his chest. I paid him no never mind. My whole body tingled, and happily it wasn't because of an upset stomach. When he finally finished breakfast, which took him longer to eat than on any other day, I quickly cleaned the dishes, straightened the bed, put my shoes on, and sat in the chair by the window with my purse nestled in my lap. I watched him as he slowly washed up and got dressed.

I glided to the door as soon as he'd finished putting on his shoes. My hand hovered over the old glass doorknob for a moment; somewhere in the back of my mind I thought, "This is Henry's door to open. I should remove my hand and step aside." Then an image of Miss Parker took hold of my consciousness—I swung the door wide open. Henry let out a grunt, like one of those ugly hogs back on the farm when they were disturbed by my brother trying to clean slop out of the pigsty.

The outside air was fragrant and warm. I stood on the sidewalk, stretched my neck back to the sky, and let the sun wash over me. A slight breeze brushed against my clothing, and I took deep breaths to fill my lungs with this new air, as though I could store it up for later use. The brick rowhouses that stretched on both sides of the street looked like elegant ladies-in-waiting. I made a mental note of the convenience store on the corner, which was probably where Henry purchased paper, envelopes, and food, and counted the number of cars parked on the opposite side of the street. I imagined myself sitting in the passenger side of one, waving to women passing by. I shaded my eyes from the sun to look up at the window where occasionally I would see a small child peeking out at me as I daydreamed my hours away. Then I looked at my own window and wondered what the child thought about me—sitting alone day after day, gazing out, framed by glass, wood, and brick.

"We have an appointment at the hairdresser. If we don't move along, we'll be late," Henry said.

"How far? It's wonderful out here, Henry."

"Not far, around the corner. Just the neighborhood, Nell; no big deal."

"Maybe for you. For me it's a universe to explore, people to observe, so much to see."

"Stay close to me. It's not a place for my woman to be alone—ever." He grabbed my arm and quickened his pace. It was only when we arrived at the hairdresser that he let go to usher me inside.

*Virginia's* was the name stenciled on the glass window of the beauty salon. We were greeted by a large woman with straightened black hair tied in a tight bun on the top of her head, wearing a pink blouse over a straight black skirt. "Hello, help you?" She looked at us in a friendly yet guarded way.

"I made an appointment for my wife, Nell. She needs her hair done."

The woman looked me up and down as if I were a new farm animal that she was deciding whether or not to purchase. I suddenly became aware of my old dress, ugly shoes, scarf tied around my head to hide my unkempt hair. Then I looked at the other women in the shop. Their faces were smooth and dazzling; eyeliner and eye shadow shimmered against their skin, catching the light as they chatted; ruby-red lipstick perfectly traced full elegant lips; their nails were long and shiny with polish, making their fingers look as though they belonged on an ivory keyboard tapping tunes. Their clothes were as colorful as their makeup and as stylish as the hairdos being pulled apart and put back together by the salon women expertly working away. I stared at the ground and felt my cheeks burn. I wanted to back out, walk away with Henry, but he stepped forward and said, "Do the best you can."

The woman made a "humph" sound, rolled her eyes at Henry, took my shoulders, and said, "Let me get a good look at your face and hair." She moved my head from side to side and undid the scarf, then tried to fluff up my braids. What had once been curled bangs on my forehead had become a mass of tight, coarse strands sticking out every which way. I tried to smooth the bangs down, but the hair sprang out again as if it had a mind of its own. "You sit right over here; I'll bring out your beauty in no time at all. I'm Virginia— friends call me Ginny."

Henry moved toward one of the empty chairs in front of a table where magazines were nestled in a fan-like pattern, but as he got ready to lower himself, the women stopped what they were doing, turned, and looked at him. Their eyes bore down on him as if he were a target with their eyes the missiles, locked onto him. He stopped before his bottom touched the chair, looked around at the women, and decided to leave, saying, "Well, guess I'll be back later to pick up my wife, Ginny."

"That's a good idea," Ginny said. "It'll be about an hour or two—and the name's *Virginia*."

"Yes, ma'am," Henry said, and he walked away, twiddling his hat.

"What's your name again, hon?" Ginny asked.

"Nell Bight."

"Live in the neighborhood?"

"Yes. Moved here a few months back."

"Where's your family from?"

"Louisiana, a small farm in a small town."

"What brought you all the way to Boston?"

"Got married. Henry has family here."

"Are they in the neighborhood?"

"Don't know. I haven't met them."

"Well, like I said, I'm Ginny. This here's Mabel, that's Josie. This is my place, and they've been working here since I opened over ten years ago." She pointed to the two stylists, who nodded but kept focused on their customers.

Ginny undid my braids and tried to get a comb through my tangled mass of hair, then gave up and used her fingers to separate the knots as best she could. She smoothed my hair down with her palms, pulling it back off my forehead so the widow's peak in my hairline was prominent. "That's a nice feature, you shouldn't hide it under bangs. Ever have your hair straightened?"

"No. Momma said I was too young, that braids were all I needed."

"What'd you want?"

"I don't know, I never thought about it."

"What about your husband?"

"Don't think my hair matters much to him."

"Here's what I'm gonna do—cut your hair into a nice shape, straighten it with this hot iron, get rid of the braids, and give you a wet set. Then you'll sit under the hairdryer, and then I'll finish up with a new fashionable style. Okay?"

"Yes, I guess so."

I settled into the large black chair, the pink cloth that Ginny tied at the back of my neck covering my whole upper body, so that only my head stuck out. It was as though the rest of me had suddenly disappeared. The reflection of Ginny in the mirror over my left shoulder; the sound of Josie and Mabel chatting about their everyday goings-on; the scent of grease and burning hair singed by the hot straightening iron —all these brought me back home. My eyes drifted shut, and I could see myself sitting on the floor between Momma's legs, my hair loose and sticking out like a ball of wool. Momma would use her fingers to part the hair and apply grease to my scalp. She'd begin to braid, starting in the back and working her way to the top of my head. I would hear my brothers' wives in the kitchen humming while doing their chores; Momma would tell me, "Sit still," as I fidgeted whenever she pulled on a particularly tight knot. The scent of our summer garden would float in through the window, promising fresh vegetables for the dinner table and provisions of canned foods for the winter months.

Suddenly I could feel Ginny shaking my shoulder. She was saying, "Nell, you okay?" My chin was slumped down, my face soaked with tears, my nose running something awful. I looked at myself in the mirror and let out a gut-wrenching wail: "I want my Momma! I want to go home!" I grabbed a hold of Ginny's arm, buried my face in her warm thick flesh, and sobbed uncontrollably.

She rubbed my shoulder, made a *shush* sound, and said, "You just need to let it all out. See this all the time. Young ones like you, move up here from the South to the big city, only to end up lonely and homesick. It'll pass, you'll find your way." She rocked me from side to side and patted my shoulder until I calmed down.

"Ginny, I've bottled up this loneliness for so long. It's

like a weed growing all over my body. I barely know who I am, what I'm supposed to do. I'm scared most of the time. No one to talk to or be with, baby on the way, all by myself. I need my family something bad."

"We'll be your new family. This here's a place for women; we look out for each other, understand?"

"Gonna be sick!" I covered my mouth with one hand, clutched my stomach with the other, and hopped out of the chair.

"Over there," Ginny said, pointing to the bathroom.

"Think it's morning sickness?" Josie asked.

"I'd say it's *husband* sickness. Did you see how he treated her? Poor thing, just a baby herself," Mabel remarked.

Ginny said, "My guess—it's both."

I slammed the bathroom door shut, propped myself up at the sink, and waited. I could feel hot blood coursing through my veins, forcing its way to my fingertips, causing them to expand and contract, getting bigger and thicker. My shoulders sagged against my heavy breathing; it felt as though my stomach were being pushed against my spine as it twisted in torturous pain. Sweat rolled down my forehead; throbbing blood vessels caused my arms to bend in muscle spasms until I looked like a sumo wrestler poised for attack. But I had no energy or willpower to move. The hollowness filling my heart and the strange life consuming my belly were on the verge of forcing me to throw up my breakfast. I hung my head in the toilet.

When the spasms stopped, I stood in front of the door, rocking back and forth and rolling on my ankles like a little doll perched on top of a car dashboard. I didn't want to go out and face the women.

Ginny tapped on the door and said, " Nell, you coming out?"

I took several deep breaths, wiped my face with a paper towel, closed my eyes tight, and saw an image of Daddy and Momma. The thought of them almost made me let out another sob; then Miss Parker came into view, and I took another deep breath and said, "Be right there." Once in the outer room I sat back down and looked at the floor. "Sorry. I don't know what came over me. Must be the baby."

"No need for sorry, it happens. I've got to get to work, though. Your husband'll back anytime, and I'm gonna have you looking beautiful."

I settled back in the chair and let Ginny do whatever she wanted to my hair. When she placed me under the hairdryer with tightly rolled curlers tugging my scalp, I welcomed the noise of the dryer, which drowned out all sounds in the room; it was peaceful, having the hot air circle my head and watching the women in conversations I couldn't hear. Thirty minutes later, I was back in the chair for Ginny's final styling. She turned me away from the mirror while she worked, saying she wanted to surprise me.

Finally she turned me to face the mirror. I didn't know who I was looking at. The woman in the mirror resembled me, but her hair was styled in a modern way, like the pictures of women in magazines. I turned my head from side to side, touched the waves on the top of my head that led to fancy curls alongside each ear. My hair was smooth, shiny, and so straight. Ginny gave me a hand mirror so I could see the back. There were even more waves going down my neck.

"Ginny!"

"Like it?"

"I don't recognize *me*."

"One more thing." She took out a makeup case and dabbed rouge on my cheeks and lips. "There, you're lovely."

Josie said, "Beautiful's more like it."

"Amazing what we find under braids and kink," Mabel added.

My neck began to turn red; tender heat traveled up all the way to the tip of my ears. "Thank you," I whispered.

When Henry walked in he looked right at me but didn't seem to actually see me.

"Henry," I said. "What do you think?"

For a brief moment his eyes reminded me of the eyes that had peered into mine during the romance-filled afternoons and evenings of our courtship. Those eyes had held the reflection of fields, wide blue skies, a promise of a love-filled future. Suddenly, as if a curtain had closed, his eyes became dark and cold, like a tin of shoe polish. He looked at my hair and said, "Braids gone? I liked your braids. I thought you were having them redone, not cut off."

Ginny, Josie and Mabel stared at him.

He glanced at them, then turned to me and said, "Looks good. We need to go."

As he pushed me out the door, Ginny yelled, "Henry, Nell will need to come back on a regular basis, for the up-keep of her hair."

Over his shoulder he said, "Yes, ma'am."

"Which way's the library?" I asked when we got outside.

"Too late for that."

"Why?"

"Hair took longer than I thought. No time now."

"Henry, you promised!"

"Another time. Let's go home."

"No."

Henry stopped and glared at me. I stared back and saw my reflection in the window behind him. I didn't recognize the woman looking back at me; she appeared much older than I felt, more sophisticated too. "I really want to go," I said in a soothing voice. "It'll make me feel better. My stomach got a little upset in the beauty shop, and I got a headache too."

"My baby okay?" He reached out to rub the little baby bump.

"Yes. Fresh air feels good; it settles me. And you know how happy books make me."

"Okay, let's go, but we won't stay long." He didn't look me in the eye as he spoke, just kept rubbing my belly.

The library was a few blocks from Ginny's shop. I made a mental note of how to get from our apartment to Ginny's and then to the library.

The massive stairs leading to the library door were filled with young people reading or chatting with one another, as though the steps were benches inviting those passing by to sit for a spell. Across the street was a large tree-lined park, the flower gardens filled with tulips and daffodils in full bloom. People were lounging on park benches, stretched out on the grass, playing with dogs, or simply enjoying an afternoon nap. It reminded me of the church picnics we enjoyed after the baptism ceremonies at the river. Everyone would gather to celebrate a young one embracing the Lord with food, laughter, and thankfulness. I caught myself nearly turning to join the strangers who, at that moment, felt more like family than the man at my side; instead, I walked inside with Henry.

The deep, musky aroma in the library filled my nostrils; I stood still, closed my eyes, and let the scent drift down to my lungs. When I opened my eyes, the lady at the counter was looking at me, a slight smile at her lips. Henry said, "I'll be over there while you get some books. Don't be long." I went to my corner, the same spot I had visited the first time, alongside the window with the rows of study desks. All the spots were taken, so I walked up and down the aisles, running my fingers against the spine of books and randomly deciding which ones to take based on how the material felt against my hand.

Henry had dozed off in the chair. I went to the counter to ask the lady a question: "Is there a children's section here?"

"Children's books are downstairs," she said.

"Do you have a reading circle for children?"

"Do you mean a children's program?"

"Yes, where adults read aloud to children and listen to the children read?"

"We certainly do, particularly on weekends and in the afternoons, after school. Do you have children?"

"No, my first is on the way. I like to read aloud, though, and I thought maybe, if you can use a volunteer..." I peeked over my shoulder to make certain Henry was still asleep.

"Come back Wednesday. You can speak to the director of our children's programs and work something out with her." She checked out my two books and handed them to me. "By the way, your hair looks nice."

"Thank you. I just came from Ginny's—she did my hair."

"Ginny does everyone's hair."

I went over to nudge Henry awake. "I'm ready, I have my books," I said.

"Yeah, let's go home."

"To the store next. I need paper for writing letters."

"It's late."

"I need paper," I said as I rubbed the baby bump.

"I guess it's near our apartment. . . . All right, but you need to get dinner ready right after."

We retraced our steps out of the library, past Ginny's shop, and back down the street toward the apartment. I glanced at myself in every window that provided a reflection of the new me and touched my hairdo as I held tight to the books.

Once at the store, I stood in the doorway and looked at everything before stepping in. *John's* was the name stenciled on the door. A little bell hanging from the top of the doorframe chimed when the door opened. A small deli counter stood to the left, holding cut cheeses, lunch meat, mixed salads, and pastries. To the right was a collection of bins holding penny candies sorted by type—red and black licorice in one bin, fireballs in another, chocolate items in yet another, and assorted hard candies overflowing in a fourth. Potato chips and popcorn packages hung from clips at the front of the first aisle. On the shelves were packaged goods like macaroni, rice, soups, cereals, seasonings, and various kinds of beans, both canned and uncooked. Fresh milk and raw meat were located in the cold container next to the candy bins, and a small collection of produce was available alongside them. Cleaning products and paper items were in the back of the store, along with a limited supply of things like writing pens, pencils, envelopes, notebooks, and paper.

"Here's the paper," Henry said. I picked out several pads of yellow lined paper. "Need that much?"

"Yes," I said. "I have to keep writing letters."

At the cash register the man greeted Henry: "Hello, Henry, how's your day?"

"Just fine, John," Henry said. I waited for him to introduce me, but he just fished in his pocket for the money to pay.

"This here the missus?" John asked.

"Yeah, my wife, Nell."

"Hello, Nell, good to meet you. How do you like the neighborhood?"

"Just fine," I said.

"Hope to see you here again," John said to me.

"Me too," I replied.

Henry said, "We gotta go."

Our apartment building was just a short walk from John's store. I stopped at the foot of the stairs leading to the front door of our building. Fresh air, neighbors sitting on the stoop chatting, the sound of cars passing by, all were a comfort to me. I held tightly to the railing and slowly eased myself up the stairs, as though it were the weight of the baby growing inside me that caused me to linger. Henry had already turned the key in the lock to our apartment before I made it to the top step. "Come on, Nell," he shouted.

After dinner I sat down to write a letter to my parents. This time I told them all about my adventure outside for the day—how beautiful my new hairdo looked and how Ginny's shop reminded me of Momma and her women friends sharing stories while quilting. I talked about the park across from the library and the people enjoying a lovely day, with spring coming to a close and offering the promise of warm summer days; I explained how this made me think about the blooming magnolias, the vegetables in our garden, the first signs of corn stalks sprouting in the fields. I described the scent of the library, the feel of the books on my fingertips, the row of desks along the window that looked like the ones we had in Miss Parker's class. After hesitating for a moment, I decided to share that it might be possible for me to work in the library, as a volunteer, with young children. Then I wrote about the constant stirring in my belly. I knew they'd want to hear how the baby was coming along.

# Chapter Eight

I STOOD AT THE DOOR, READY TO OPEN IT AND HEAD outside. After a quick look around the apartment and several deep breaths, I turned the knob and quickly snuck out. The spare key that had been hidden in Henry's top drawer made a scratching sound as it turned in the lock. I looked from side to side, afraid that someone might hear me escaping who would report back to Henry.

"Hi, Ginny," I said ten minutes later, while opening the door to her shop.

"Nell. Back so soon?"

"On the way to the library—thought I'd stop and visit."

"Henry with you?"

"No."

"He know you out and about?"

"No."

"Good for you. Come on in, let me look at your hair. Held up nicely. I can freshen it a bit."

"No, thank you. I did what you showed me to keep the style. It's been four days, and it still looks good."

"Come Saturday you'll want to come back for a fresh wash and set."

"Maybe."

"What's going on at the library?"

"I'm speaking to them about volunteering—with the children, being a reader."

"You good with books and numbers?"

"Yes, always the best in my class back home."

"Maybe we can work up a bartering system: you can have your hair done regularly for doing paperwork for me. Interested?"

"Sounds good, but I'm not sure. Though my momma and the neighbors had arrangements like that, and it worked for them."

"Think about it—could work for us too."

"Okay. Gotta go, bye."

"Nell—careful."

"Ma'am?"

"Some men don't take kindly to a woman breaking out on her own. You be careful."

"Yes, ma'am," I said, while backing out the door.

The walk from Ginny's to the library seemed shorter than it had on Saturday. This was a weekday morning, so fewer people were strolling around and almost no one was lounging in the park across the street from the library. My feet felt light as I climbed the steps to the big door. As I approached the counter, I realized that the pounding in my chest and the quiver in my belly weren't bothersome feelings today. I was on my own, a new adventure in the making. Ginny's parting words, however, held tight in the back of my mind, like a bad dream I'd yet to experience.

Irene, the lady at the counter, smiled when she saw me and said, "Nell, you came. I'll get Susan; she runs the children's program." She stepped into the office and came back with another woman. "Susan, this is Nell. She's interested in being a volunteer. Nell, Susan." Irene made the introductions, and then Susan led me to the children's area downstairs.

Color—that was the first thing that struck me when we walked to the lower floor: primary colors splashed on everything in the room. The children's books were facing out on the shelves, the covers in full view, with characters or animals in motion. Four-legged wooden chairs, no taller than my knees, were scattered around the room; each had a red, blue, yellow, and black leg; the seats were painted brown, and the seat backs were a natural light wood stain. All the letters of the alphabet hung around the top of the wall on a banner, with a colorful character or item drawn alongside each—from a juicy red apple at A to an elegant zebra at Z. Sunlight streamed through the large windows, casting an inviting glow—something I hadn't expected, since this was the lower level, but the high ceiling welcomed daylight through the glass.

A sturdy carpet covered the entire floor; squares of different colors danced across the room, with built-in games for the children to play: hopscotch, tic-tac-toe, twister, even puzzles with moveable pieces. Near one of the windows a circle of chairs were arranged around one larger chair. "Is this where the reading takes place?" I asked Susan.

"Yes, the leader gets to use the big chair, although it's much smaller than one an adult would normally sit in. It's better if the children see us at the same level as themselves; they respond better."

"Children must love this place," I said.

"It's taken me three years to get the program up and running. Now we can't keep people away—it's always full of youngsters, especially on weekends. So you'd like to volunteer?"

"Yes. I love books and am a good reader, and I thought that if you need readers, I could help out."

"Where did you finish high school?"

"I didn't—I got married and moved here from Louisiana in April. I was good in school, but didn't finish. Is that a problem?"

"No. Love of books, being a good reader, and being good with children are what matters most. Why don't you pick up a book and read a little to me?"

I chose *The Little Engine That Could* and read a couple of pages.

Susan stopped me right away. "Nice reading voice," she said. "Children will respond to your enthusiasm; your love of words comes out nicely as you read. Saturday is our busiest day; can you come then?"

"Saturday isn't good for me—I don't think I can get away."

"Wednesdays are good too. We have a group that comes in at lunchtime, kindergarten and first graders who have an early end to the school day. They'll be arriving shortly. Can you stay today and then come back every week on Wednesday?"

"Yes," I said. My skin tingled. It was all I could do not to jump up and down in glee, even though I knew I'd have to figure out what to say to Henry about this—if anything at all.

When the children arrived for the reading, Susan asked me how I'd like to be introduced to them. I said, "They can call me Mrs. Bight."

I stopped by Ginny's on the way home and told her, Mabel, and Josie about my experience at the library and the new volunteer job. All three of them nodded as they looked at one another. "Remember what I said, about being careful," Ginny reminded me.

"I know, and I will be, but I need to do this for me. Sometimes you just have do what's in your heart, you know?"

"Don't have to tell me," Josie said.

"Me neither," Mabel added.

"We all agree," said Ginny. "A little caution can help, though. What'll you tell Henry?"

"Thought maybe I'd take you up on your bartering offer, make Wednesdays my regular day here and go to the library too. That way Henry won't have to walk me here on Saturdays and wait. Does that sound good?"

"Works for me," Ginny said. "Now all you have to do is sell it to Henry. Good luck with that!"

I rushed home to prepare meatloaf and get ready for my conversation with Henry. Once the food was prepared, I took special care to have the table looking pretty, with a freshly cleaned and pressed cloth covering the dented wood and our places set with plates, forks, and knives lined up neatly across from each other. I placed my little box from the dresser in the center of the table for decoration, but then decided to remove it. The windows were cracked open to allow the springtime air to move the aroma of food around.

Henry walked in the door exactly at six o'clock as always. The meatloaf was done, along with baked sweet potatoes and green beans. I had kept the food warm on the stove but was ready to serve him as soon as he took off his shoes and cleaned up for dinner.

"Smells good," he said. "I'm hungry."

"Have your favorite meal, ready whenever you are."

I fidgeted at the stove while he dusted and lightly buffed his shoes. Once he sat down, I placed the food in the center of the table and joined him. We bowed our heads in silence to say grace. Then he reached for the food and filled his plate. I waited for him to take what he wanted and then served myself. After several mouthfuls, he mumbled, "Good."

I picked at my food, waiting for the best moment to tell him about my plan. "Henry, you remember how Ginny said I'd need to go back every Saturday for my hair?"

"Humph."

"Well, I talked to Ginny today."

"What do you mean? You left the apartment?"

"Yes, I did."

"I told you never to go out alone, didn't I?"

"Yes, Henry, but I thought, since it's not far, and it was a nice day . . . and the clean air settled my stomach. Here, rub the baby for a moment." I walked over so he could touch the baby bump. "That feels good," I said. "Don't know what it is, but as soon as I get fresh air my stomach settles right down. It's as though the baby knows he needs space and clean air to grow and be healthy. Anyway, I thought I could go to Ginny's on Wednesdays, have my hair done. That way you don't have to go with me on Saturdays and wait; that's her busiest day. But Wednesdays are pretty quiet. I can get there in no time, have my hair done, and be back to have a meal ready for you, like tonight. Maybe Wednesdays'll be meat-loaf every week. Would you like that?"

"Could work. I still don't like the idea of you being out by yourself."

"But it's good for me, and for your baby. You know I

need help to understand about having a baby. Ginny and Mabel are mothers—they know things. I'd turn to Momma if I could. I need to talk about pregnancy, birthing, and mothering, so I'm certain to do the right things for your baby."

"I'll think on it."

"Thank you," I said.

After dinner, dishes cleaned, Henry finished polishing his shoes, and I walked over to him and slid my arms around his waist. We hadn't enjoyed sex since the doctor had confirmed my pregnancy. "Henry, the doctor said it's okay to have sex while I'm pregnant, at least in the early stages." I slid my hands to his private parts, slowly rubbing in a circular motion. He leaned his body into me and began to moan. Our clothing fell to the floor. Henry sat on the bed, I stood in front of him, and he pressed his face against my belly, put his lips on my growing breasts, ran his hands up and down my body. "Missed this," he said. Our bodies curled into comfortable movements on top of the quilt. Afterward we fell into a deep sleep, the room laced with the scent of our sex.

WHEN I ARRIVED at Ginny's the next Wednesday morning at ten o'clock, the shop's opening time, she and the girls were getting ready for the day: turning on lights, placing supplies out, running the faucets to bring up warm water, dusting the counters, watering the plants in the windows, and arranging reading material on the table. I walked in and said to Ginny, "I'll be here every Wednesday! If that's okay with you."

"Okay by me. Like I told you, I can use help with paperwork and you can get your hair done; it's a fair trade."

"I can pay. Henry gave me money, but I'll still help you."

"You hold onto that money—we'll keep our arrangement. A woman should always have a little something of her own hidden away."

I was happy to be in the shop again, but what I really wanted was to make my way to the library. Ginny was quick with my hair, and then she showed me how I could help her with organizing paperwork and filing receipts. She asked me if I could answer the phone and handle appointments. "Never used a phone," I had to admit. That caused all three women to raise their eyebrows and stare at me. "Daddy never wanted a phone, said it was troublesome to have that kind of thing around. One farmer nearby had a phone; he claimed whenever it rang his chickens got agitated and wouldn't lay eggs. Daddy didn't want to go through that. Momma wanted one. She thought it would be important, but she couldn't get Daddy to agree, so if Momma wanted to make a call, she went to the neighbors' house. That didn't happen often."

"But what about in your apartment here?" Mabel asked.

"Henry said we don't need a phone."

Josie explained the phone and how to make notes in the appointment book. I sat at the little desk, did my chores, and watched as customers began to arrive for their appointments. I was mesmerized by the stylists' hands, the easy way they worked both hair and equipment while chatting away. It reminded me of Momma and the women at home—they had the same musical rhythm to their gestures and soothing sound to their voices; their hands were nimble and expert at every task. It was as though each woman played a jazz instrument with her fingers and created an unforgettable tune with her voice.

My walk to the library was quick. I barely noticed the people on the street, cars passing by, or activity in the shops. As soon as I stepped through the library's big doors, my heart began to flutter. I paused for a moment to savor the scent inside and take in the beauty of the main room. Then, after waving to Irene, I headed downstairs.

Children had already arrived. They looked up as I walked in and said, almost in unison, "Hello, Mrs. Bight." I stood up tall, took a deep breath, straightened my shoulders, and greeted the children with a smile. They gathered in a circle in the chairs, each holding a copy of the book I had chosen for the day's reading.

Miss Parker had started each of our reading sessions at school with a description of the story and then read a few lines aloud before asking the class to read for her. I did the same. The children listened to my voice in rapt silence, their faces filled with earnestness. I stopped reading after the first paragraph to look at them. "Who would like to read now?"

Several hands flew into the air, but there was one girl to my left who waved her hand so frantically that she lifted herself off the chair and bounced up and down. I nodded to her; she jumped up and began to read. Her voice was strong, each word pronounced with care and understanding. If she came to a word she was unsure about, she broke it down into syllables and spoke each one as though it stood on its own, then put it all together as one word. She didn't want to stop, but eventually I thanked her and let others read. No one was as proficient as the first girl, but each had a turn.

The hour sped by. Parents arrived to gather their children, and I prepared to leave and make my way home. Karen, the first reader, came up to me and said, "Mrs. Bight,

I liked hearing you read. I love to read. Thank you, bye." At that moment I realized what had drawn me to this child— this is what I must have looked like to Miss Parker.

After dinner Henry said, "Hair looks good. You went straight to the hairdressers, then back home?"

"Yes," I said without hesitation.

There was so much I wanted to share in my letter home that night, about the library and my new friends at Ginny's. I described how the children were playful but always attentive when it was time to read stories; that hearing the children call me "Mrs. Bight" warmed my heart; how each child had a different reading ability, so I was careful to make sure they felt comfortable when it was their turn; and how reading to them and hearing their small voices reminded me of Miss Parker's class; I hoped that the children would learn as much from me as I had from her.

I recounted how the walk to Ginny's on feet that had outgrown shoes, with ankles that craved a cool splash of water and a belly that grew with every step, was sometimes difficult but always enjoyable; and how the sweat on my forehead and dappled stains on the fabric of my dress at the armpits made me think of home. I reminisced about summers in Louisiana, as I adjusted to summers in the North. Back home, thick June heat would have heralded the arrival of stifling summer hotness. I remembered how it would descend upon the roads, creating dust that clung to my sweaty body like a second layer of skin. I wrote that summer in Boston wasn't much different, except for the hard surfaces. The sun beat down on the concrete, bouncing heat back into my face. The spring flowers along the sidewalk began to wilt for want of regular rain. At night I'd open the windows in the apartment, hoping to feel a breeze wash some of the dankness out, but the curtains stayed limp; the air just didn't want to move. Our bedsheets felt as though dryness weren't meant to be, no matter how long I let them hang on the line after washing. Yet unlike home, I didn't have a front porch to provide solace from the inside swelter, a place to sit with family and friends, sharing stories or comfortable silence.

Ginny and the girls were easy to write about; it was as though I were looking at people back home whenever I sat in the shop. I described how pretty they were, and so different too. Ginny was the "in charge" person, just like Momma. She walked into the room and a big "shush" hummed as everyone waited to hear her speak. Mabel I likened to my brother's wife, Bernice, with big shoulders and strong arms ready to provide support even when a person didn't realize she needed it. And Josie was the fun-loving girl looking forward to the next date or new adventure. Kinda like me, as far as adventure went anyway . . . the way I used to be. I wrote about their hands—how watching them work made me see how much women can do, and that our hands were alike, North or South. No matter if we were in the fields doing backbreaking chores, in the kitchen preparing to feed the family, standing in a classroom sharing knowledge, making the local women beautiful in shop chairs, or quilting on the porch with special pieces of fabric—our hands danced.

I ended as I always did, with "I love you, your Baby Girl." Then I sat quietly by the window, clutched the letter to my chest, and tried to block out the sound of Henry's snoring.

## Chapter Nine

I STOOD AT THE TOP OF THE STAIRS AND STARED DOWN at the ice and slush that had found a home on every inch of the steps and the sidewalk. My back ached, and my stomach protruded so much that only the tips of my shoes were visible to my weary eyes. Somehow I needed to steady myself, hold my back, and rub my belly at the same time, as I gingerly inched down each step.

The first time it snowed had been magical. None of the descriptions in my books came close to the real experience of seeing white flakes fill the air, gently gliding down, dusting the windowsill with shimmery crystals that formed delicate mounds. But moving about while seven months pregnant on the aftermath of snow—ice, slush, cold puddles—was anything but beautiful. I wanted to make my way down the stairs, along the slippery sidewalk, and into Ginny's shop without falling and rolling along the street like an out-of-control, overstuffed sausage.

Ginny noticed me as I crept up to the door, holding tight to the wall outside. She rushed to greet me. "You all right?"

I shuffled beside her as she helped me inside and led me to the nearest chair, where I sat with a thump. "Getting harder and harder to walk at all, never mind on slippery sidewalks." I held tight to my stomach as I spoke; the baby was kicking as if to tell me he finally felt safe too, now that I was warm and not moving about like a drunken sailor.

"Best be careful," Ginny said. "You take a fall, and it's you *and* the baby that could suffer."

"Was thinking on the way here that I may need to stay close to home from now on. Baby's due in about eight weeks. It pains me to think about not coming out on Wednesdays, seeing all of you, reading to the children, but . . . I don't know . . . I may need to stop."

"You'll still see us," Josie said. "We'll come by your place to visit. See how you're doing."

"Not sure that'll work. Henry won't want me to have visitors."

"We'll come anyway, when he's out. On Wednesdays— we'll keep the same day as now, at lunch time, and take turns so one of us is always here to handle the shop."

Mabel nodded in agreement as both she and Josie continued working on their customers' hair.

"I'll miss the children. They're such a treat. Last week they surprised me with a baby shower. Brought in hand-made cards and a few gifts—a rattle, a pacifier, a crocheted blanket, and the cutest little infant booties. It was nice of their mothers to think about me. But I had to leave everything there, in a storage box." I didn't want to cry, but that first tear fell from my chin onto the desk, and suddenly my eyes were so full of moisture that I lost sight of my friends and the room.

Ginny rubbed my shoulders, saying, "Just let it out. You're a jumble of emotions right now. It happens to all expecting women. Your mind and body, not your own."

"Gonna miss y'all." I squeezed Ginny's hand as she continued to rub my shoulders.

"You heard Josie, we'll visit." But the tone in Ginny's voice belied the assurance of her words.

Finished with the paperwork for the day, I slowly put my coat, hat, and gloves on—the newest clothing I owned, which Henry had brought home one day, telling me to "keep my baby warm when you're outdoors." Ginny had touched up my hair for what I feared would be the last time. I looked around the shop and took in the smells of hair being cleaned and styled with fancy products designed to enhance a woman's beauty. I hoped that a permanent imprint of this magical world would be stenciled on my mind.

Gentle snowflakes were brushing against the lettering that spelled *Ginny's* backwards, when you looked from this side of the glass out at the street. The icy sidewalk looked terrifying again. I began to envision my walk to the library— holding onto walls, parked cars, light poles—praying to God that I wouldn't slip and fall. And then the stairs up to the library's front doors, steep and slick—it was going to be so difficult. I'd tell Susan when the children left that this would be my last day for a while. At least until after the baby was born and I was able to get around with him. Maybe not until the spring.

Ginny interrupted my reverie. "Before you go, we have something for you."

She went to the back storage room and rolled out the most beautiful baby carriage, with a big red ribbon tied to the handle bar. The girls gathered around me, each giving me a big hug and kiss on my cheek. "You'll need this for your walks with the baby, once winter lets up," she said.

I touched the deep blue cloth on the bonnet of the carriage and ran my hands along the inside, which was cushioned with soft silky fabric and equipped with a little pillow and blanket. "It's lovely," I said, more to myself then to them. "Thank you, but I can't take it to the apartment."

"Don't you worry 'bout that," Josie said. "We decided to keep it here until the baby's born. We'll just bring it over on one of our visits. Tell Henry it's our gift to you. We got a plan." There was a defiance in her voice that gave me little comfort.

After my reading session at the library ended, I said good-bye to the children, tidied the room, and wistfully looked around the space that had become more home to me than the apartment. Then I took one long last deep breath of the book-scented air, turned, and headed out the front door of the library.

My head was bent low, to fend off the snow that was coming down fast and thick and to make certain of my footing on the wet steps. I saw the tips of his shoes before I heard him bellow at me.

"Nell! What the hell you doing here?" He grabbed my arm in a vise-like grip.

"Henry!" I couldn't move. The steps began to whirl beneath me; it felt as though I were suddenly seeing double, my eyes playing tricks on me. "I . . ."

"You what? Stepping out on me, lying!" He pressed his face into mine. Steam flowed from his flared nostrils as he gripped my arm more and more tightly. His expression reminded me of the way the mean hogs had looked in the pen; they'd attack at the slightest provocation, and we knew to stay away whenever the animals took on that look.

"I . . ." Only moans emitted from my tightened throat.

At that moment the library door opened and several of the children bounded out, with their mothers at their side. "Bye, Mrs. Bight, we'll miss you," they said in unison. I limply waved to them. Their mothers glanced at me, concern flashing across their faces. Then they looked away and quickly moved on past Henry and me.

"How they know you?" Henry hissed in my face, pulling me closer to him.

"I read . . . volunteer . . . Wednesdays."

"That's over! Understand?"

"But . . ."

He yanked my arm and tugged me within an inch of his nose, so that we were facing off like two boxers preening for the cameras before the big fight. "No more hairdresser either. Understand?"

"Henry, stop it. You're hurting me," I pleaded. "You'll hurt your baby!" My head was reeling. I didn't recognize this Henry. He'd been replaced by a manic animal on the verge of strangling me.

"Stay home, do as I say. Understand?"

My body felt limp, as though it had been drained of blood, its bones reduced to mush, my heart wrenched out with a knife. Cold was seeping into my feet, through the sleeves of my coat, and down my neck. "Yes, Henry," was all I could manage in response to his anger.

Fiercely pulling on my arm, he rushed me down the stone stairs. I slipped from one snow-laden tread to another, practically falling with each jerky motion. We sped along the sidewalk like two people trying to catch a departing train. When we approached Ginny's shop, I bent my chin deep into the top of my coat collar. *No*, I silently begged, *keep going.* But he stopped right in front of the window, just stood there glaring at my friends until they noticed us. I wanted to melt into the snow gathering around my shoes, become a puddle that would dry up and disappear in the next day's sunlight.

"Nell, you okay?" Ginny poked her head out the door.

I just shook from side to side, without looking up.

"You sure?" she asked.

"This here *my* wife!" Henry shouted, and shoved me toward Ginny and the shop window, never letting go of my upper arm. "She do as *I* say. You put things in her head. No more!"

I heard Ginny walk out and the door close behind her. She said in her most controlled and in-charge voice, "Nell's my friend. We look out for our friends around here." The tips of her shoes were almost touching the tips of Henry's shoes.

"She's my wife. Coming home, not leaving. You stay away, woman. You hear me!"

She stepped toward Henry, closing the gap between the tips of their shoes. Then she began to speak to me, but she never took her eyes off of him. "Nell, I'm gonna come around your way, just to visit. It'll be unannounced, since you don't have a phone. But the girls and I *will* visit. And if it ever looks like you in any kind of trouble, any at all, or if you don't answer when we knock on door, then I want you to know that I'll call the police. I'll just ask them to look in on you, make sure you're okay, what with being alone and pregnant and all. Remember—I *will* call the police." She touched my shoulder on the side that wasn't numb from pain and lack of circulation.

Henry made a guttural hog sound and dragged me down the street toward our apartment. I never looked up, just groaned as he dragged me away.

# Chapter Ten

THERE WAS A KNOCK ON THE DOOR. I WASN'T SURE if the sound was just in my mind, since unsettled sleep had given way to delusions in the morning. I squirmed in bed, clutched the blankets to my chest hoping for some warmth, and tried to let sleep take hold again. I heard the knock again, through the haze of a sleeping-waking state, at the same moment that the first contraction gripped my insides.

The pounding on the door was overshadowed by the screams of pain that rushed from my throat with the next contraction. I pumped quick breaths of air from my lungs and out my mouth, the way the doctor's nurse had showed me during the last office visit: "Do this when you feel the first jolt; it'll help you manage the pain and relax your muscles." She had demonstrated the process and watched me as I mimicked the breathing technique. "Good," she'd said. "You got it."

But she hadn't described how searing the pain would be, how my body would want to curl into a fist but couldn't with the baby on top of all my organs, fighting to kick his way out. When the pain subsided I heard more hammering on the door and Ginny shouting, "Nell! Let us in." I rolled onto my side, pushed myself to the edge of the bed, and shuffled to the door, holding my back and stomach for balance.

"Nell! You look . . . oh my! You're in labor!"

I stared at her and then at the wet stains on my night-gown and legs. "Ginny, help!" It was all I could say before another involuntary reflex gripped my body and forced a scream so loud that my ears started to ring. "Please!"

"Lay her on the floor," Ginny said to Mabel.

"We need an ambulance!" Mabel shouted.

"Too late for that—this baby's coming now! Get the pil-lows and sheets, and check your watch; count the time be-tween contractions. Boil some water. Wipe her forehead. We're having a baby!" Ginny shouted orders to Mabel while easing me onto the floor.

"You just settle right here, Nell. I've done this before."

"But . . . Henry . . . wants his baby born in hospital," I managed to protest between the sudden bouts of pain and my forced breathing.

"Not going to happen. Don't worry about Henry. You the only concern now."

"But—" I fell back with the next muscle lurch and belted out a scream that must have shaken the walls. "Let it out!" I could feel the baby pressing against my uterus, trying to force his way into the world. "Please!" I begged Ginny.

"Not yet; if it's too soon you'll hurt yourself. Don't push! I'll tell you when."

"Momma!" I shouted at the air.

"Mabel, help me roll Nell on her side and put pressure on her back. Rub hard! Nell, keep doing the breathing; you have to hold on a little longer."

I wanted Momma, Bernice, Daddy—I wanted to grab them, hug them, shout at them. "Where are you? Why did you send me away? Why don't you answer my letters?" I sobbed into the sweat-drenched sheets, confusing my body with its labor pains and the empty ache nursing my soul. "Henry! What've you done to me?" I thumped my fists on the floor.

Ginny stuck her fingers inside me, searching around the way I remembered the midwives doing with other women back home. It had looked disgusting then to my young and curious eyes, and it felt even worse now, when I was the object of the prodding.

"Okay, I think she's ready," Ginny said. "Put her on the floor and sit behind her for support. She's gonna need it."

Mabel shifted me, straddled her legs on either side of my shoulders, and rested my head against her stomach. She dabbed my forehead with the cool cloth and kissed the top of my head. "It's okay," she said in a reassuring voice that made me think even more about my Momma. "You're with family."

The sobs came harder and harder; my mind and body were shaking as if I were in a rickety carriage barreling down a cobblestone street.

"Push!" Ginny commanded. "Push!" Mabel angled me forward as I pushed until my energy was exhausted.

"Rest a moment," Ginny said. Before I could finish a series of quick breaths, she shouted again, "Push, harder!" I pushed and suddenly felt something between my legs begin to move, stretching me open. "It's the head! One more big push!" She put force against my stomach with her hand while Mabel raised my shoulders higher. I strained so hard my eyes pressed shut, my neck muscles began to ache, and my chin seemed to meld into the top of my chest bone.

"I have his head!" Ginny took hold of the baby's head

and gently moved it from side to side, easing it out of my vagina. I could see the protruding scalp, covered with blood and ooze, as she continued to pull. When the baby's legs were free, she gathered it up and plopped him on my chest. Then she cut the cord and eased the afterbirth onto the sheets with a splash. Mabel used the damp cloth to clean his skin, wipe his eyes, and clear his mouth. The tiny thing let out a wail. I looked away, my arms limp at my side.

"Nell, hold your baby, give your breast," Ginny said with a lilt of concern in her voice.

"Not mine!" I crossed my arms over my face and yelled, "Take it away!"

"Nell!" Ginny touched my arm and tried to move it away from my face, but I held tight.

"What's wrong with her?" Mabel whispered. "Never seen a woman act this way towards her baby."

"She's not a woman, just a sixteen-year-old child herself. Scared is all . . . Nell, listen to me." Ginny stroked my damp hair with kind gentleness. Momma had soothed me in the same way whenever fear showed up, fangs exposed.

"Momma!" I groaned between gasps of air.

"You the momma now," Ginny said. She cupped her hand under my breast, slid the baby up, and slipped my nipple into its mouth. It grabbed hold and began sucking like a starving newborn calf at a cow's tit. Ginny took my arm and wrapped it around the baby's back; she rested my hand against its head, then gave me a gentle push. "This is how you hold him to your breast," she said, and let go, forcing me to keep it in place.

I kept my eyes squeezed tight and cradled the dollop of

shiny flesh in my arms, wondering how something *of* me could be so foreign *to* me.

A thin fog bedimmed my mind. It was as though I were watching from afar as Ginny and Mabel cleaned blood and muck from between my legs, tidied the room, mopped the floor, and eased me into bed, resting the baby on my chest. I let my body give in to their comforting movements, imagining myself rocking in a cloth hammock swaying between two magnolia trees, a cool Louisiana breeze brushing against my skin. But on the inside of my eyelids the mosaic of my life began to form—it resembled rivulets of birth-waste splashed on the floor.

## Chapter Eleven

APRIL WAS BORN IN APRIL. SHE WAS SUCH A CUTE baby. Her tiny face and hands reminded me of the new buds appearing on the flowering trees just beginning to wake from winter's grip. Henry didn't seem to care about her name. The day I had given birth to the first baby, just fourteen months before, Henry had grabbed the baby from my chest, held it up to the ceiling cupped in his hands, and proclaimed, "My son, Henry Junior." When he saw that this baby was a girl, with my features, he looked away without touching her and said, "Call it whatever you want."

"April," I said. "My little ray of springtime."

He said, "Humph."


I LOOKED AT Junior playing on the floor, April wiggling in the crib, and the apartment that had been getting smaller every day since the children joined us. Their two cribs were placed longways against the wall next to our bed, with just enough space for me to swing my legs out on the side of the bed and stand. It was easy to reach into April's crib at night to breastfeed her or to give Junior his bottle. Henry had moved to the side facing the bathroom, saying it would be easier for me to take care of the babies if I slept near them. He told me to be quiet at night with their needs so as not to wake him.

As I made my way to the bathroom I tripped over the things Henry had brought home for Junior the night before. In addition to the small football and basketball already taking up space, a baseball, glove, and bat had been added. I asked Henry, "Why so many things for Junior? He's too little to enjoy them. And what about April?"

He said, "My son needs to know about sports now. That way I can see where his talents are."

"And April?" I asked again.

"She's your concern," he replied.

Sometimes I tried to get Henry to take April while I washed the dishes after dinner. "Hold your daughter while I'm cleaning."

"No," he'd grunt. "I need to polish my shoes." He always tended to his shoes while I tidied up and got the children down for the night.

I was anxious for the girls to arrive today. Wednesday continued to be the one day I was able to have visitors, enjoy adult conversation, and remember that there was a life outside this tiny place the four of us called home. Henry had taken issue with the visits by Ginny, Mabel, and Josie after the horrible day he'd dragged me home as if I were a sack of potatoes he could toss around at will. But I reminded him, "If it hadn't been for Ginny, your son might not have made it into the world." He didn't complain again. Instead he brought home a small radio one day, saying, "This can keep you company, along with your books." But though I loved books, and though listening to the radio let me learn about the outside world and enjoy music, nothing could replace conversations with another woman.

"Just me today," Josie said as she came in and took a seat at the table.

"Glad you're here. How're Ginny and Mabel? How're things at the shop? Any new customers? What's the weather like out there? Hungry? I have some chili and cornbread. Meat's left over from the meatloaf I made for Henry, hope that's all right. Babies quiet right now. April loves her naps, and Junior won't bother with us—he's enjoying all the things Henry brings home for him to play with. Honestly, I don't know how much more we can fit into this place. You saw the stuff lined up in the hall outside? I have to keep the baby carriage, playpen, and highchairs there. I think the neighbors don't like it much, but no one's complained, at least not to me. When we go outside for a walk, Henry has to carry everything to the sidewalk and then come back to get me and the children. He carries Junior; April is my responsibility. I don't go without Henry; he doesn't want me to, thinks his children won't be safe. Often he takes Junior by himself, leaves April and me here. Sometimes I find myself talking to the walls, waiting for my voice to bounce back at me like another woman keeping me company. All I actually hear is children noises.

"It's good to have a radio. I listen whenever the children are quiet. Don't always understand what I hear coming from the box. Sounds like there's still trouble in the South between the races. My Daddy always said blacks built this country with our blood and whites rule over it with their fists. Made him angry, but then he'd say, 'A man can't live on a diet of hate. We have to carry on and learn to forgive.' I heard talk about something called the Olympics due to happen next summer, where athletes from all over the world come together and compete. Gonna be in Rome this time. There's excitement about a black boxer, Cassius Clay—they say he's someone to pay attention to. And a black woman runner, Wilma Rudolf, she won medals in the last games and should win again. Imagine, Blacks from America being famous all over the world. I hope to get books about them so I can learn more.

"The radio talkers are excited about the presidential election. This John Kennedy is so young, and a Catholic. They think he'll win and the country will be better for it. Even Blacks may benefit from his presidency. I'd like to ask my Daddy what he thinks. I know he and the men are chewing on this every night on the front porch. Want more tea, or chili? So glad you came to visit."

I must have been walking in circles as I went on and on. Josie finally stopped me, put her hands on my shoulders, and said, "Nell, it's all right, let's just sit and chat for a while. I have to get back to the shop in an hour—I have a new customer today. The chili looks delicious.

"I think these Olympics will be very exciting. Ginny plans to have a TV in the shop so our customers can watch the games. This will be the first time the world can see the events live, not just rely on radio announcers and day-old newspaper stories. TV is going to change everything.

"You're right about race relations. Things have changed but not necessarily for the better. Things are brewing in the South—I think Southern Blacks have had enough and the younger ones are going to lash out eventually. And here it's not that much different, we just like to fool ourselves into thinking it's better. But oppression takes a more subtle turn in the North. Just look at all the Southern Blacks migrating here, like all of us. We're forced into the same neighborhoods—not that we'd want to live in the white areas. Still, space is running out. These old brownstones are all owned by whites. They don't take care of the buildings, and we just crowd more and more people into the same dreary spaces. It's as though our people are still in slave ships, stacked one on top of the other or living in tight slave quarters on a plantation. Just look at your situation, stuck in this tiny place, two children, Henry not letting you out . . ." She abruptly stopped talking and reached to touch my cheek. "Oh, Nell, I'm sorry. Didn't mean to say that."

I picked at the hard skin around my fingernails and said, "You're right—look at me."

"Sorry. Well, I'd better be going. Ginny'll be expecting me soon." She held Junior and then April, gave them each a kiss. Then she wrapped her arms around me and held on, rocking us back and forth. "You be strong," she whispered.

After she left, I watched her on the stairs, then ran to the window to see her figure fade into the collection of people making their way along the sidewalk, happily living their lives on what seemed to be a fine spring day. I envisioned her giving a report to Ginny and Mabel once back at the shop. She'd tell them I looked weary. I'd rambled on and on about nothing in particular. She'd say that my hair was a mess. I was little more than a caged bird with a couple of chicks pecking away, my daily companions. My life was as minuscule as the apartment. When I turned away from the window and viewed my inside life, it felt as though the walls were closing in, the ceiling inching its way down onto my head, the evaporating air causing me to grasp for breath. *This is my slave ship*, I thought, *floating on stormy seas with an uncertain future on the horizon.* I sighed, took out a piece of paper, and wrote a letter home:

*Dear Mom and Dad,*
*I turned eighteen today. I love you.*
*Your Baby Girl*

# Chapter Twelve

I CONTINUED TO WRITE LETTERS HOME, ALTHOUGH THE messages got shorter and shorter once I became a momma. Almost two years had passed since I came North and started writing—and still there was no response from my family. I filled my letters with news about the children; how their appearance and behavior changed day to day; how Junior took his first steps and began constantly running around like an athlete; how April was alert to my movements and moods, her eyes following me throughout the day; how they each needed me in their own unique ways. I didn't write about Henry and how his need for me at night was relentless. I didn't want to be like my momma, my sisters, and my brothers' wives—always walking around with a round belly, one baby at my breast, one at my skirt, and my husband thinking about the next one to be made. Yet here I was. I didn't share my disappointment.

One day a letter arrived at the apartment addressed to me. It was from my momma.

*Dear Baby Girl,*

*We got all of your letters, just so you know. You seem to be very happy up North. Baby Girl, sadness has settled here with the family. Your Daddy took real ill after you left. It was sudden. We tried everything to keep him, but the Lord called Daddy up and he's no longer with us. I miss him so much. You were his special baby girl. He was happy to see you married and starting a family of your own. I know he'd want you to continue to build your family up North and keep him in your heart.*

*We buried him in the cemetery near the church, you remember. We had a good going-home ceremony for him, everyone in the county was there. I'm sorry you couldn't come. We called Henry right away. He told us you haven't been strong since having the babies and thought it best if you didn't travel so far.*

*I miss you, Baby Girl. I hope to see you one day soon and meet my new grandbabies, they look so cute, just like you. Keep writing.*

*Love,*
*Your Momma*

My legs turned into liquid. I sank to the floor, clutching my momma's message in a tight fist against my chest. The walls of the apartment began to close in on me, while the floor spun beneath my feet as though I were on a merry-go-round with ugly creatures as the rides. "*DADDY! DADDY! DADDY!*" I called, curled on my side, knees pulled to my chest, sobs lulling me into a hurtful, empty, angry coma.

April let out a wail from her crib, but the sound was little more than a faint echo of my guttural noises. Junior staggered to where I lay, stood over me, and then plopped on the floor at my shoulder, tears streaming down his face.

I was barely aware of the children. There was just one clear thought in my mind—*Henry knew!*

I wanted to get up and gather myself, but my body was frozen—a prone statue, a hard ebony carving that looked like a woman. Junior was still next to me, leaning his head against me. He never made a sound. I heard April cry, but she stopped soon, as though she knew I wouldn't take care of her needs. The little bit of sunshine that came through the window faded, slowly shifting the room from bright light into darkness.

I heard Henry open the door, heard his shoes, felt the darkness of our home expand with his presence. He fumbled as he stepped inside, eyed me on the floor, and looked at his son, motionless at my side. April let out a wail, wanting to get his attention, but he ignored her and reached for Junior. "Nell, what's wrong?"

Slowly I raised myself up to a sitting position and wiped my face on the sleeve of my crumpled dress. Then I handed him the letter still clenched in my fist.

Henry read the message from my momma and looked away. "Oh, Nell, I'm so sorry."

I raised myself onto my knees, threw my head back, spread my arms to the side, and let out a howl that pierced the walls of our apartment, nearly rattling the windows. April started screaming. "How could you?" I spit out the words between clenched teeth.

"Nell!" He tried to touch me, but I pushed his hands away.

"How?" I growled and began to hit him on his shoulders. My blows landed like soft touches rather than the hard pounding I'd intended. Junior joined me with blows on Henry's back from his tiny fists.

"Nell, I'm sorry. I should've told you." He tried to pull me close. I shoved him away.

"When did you know?"

"A few days after your daddy passed. You must've told your momma where I worked. I got a phone call. She told me then. I said it wouldn't be good for you to travel, to leave the children or take them with you. She understood. Oh, Nell, I . . ."

"Stop!" I screamed. "You bastard! He was my father."

"I didn't know what to do. Your momma said she'd send a message to you, and we decided to let her tell you in her own way."

"I should've seen my daddy buried. Been with my family. How could you take that away from me? How?"

"Nell—I—"

"You what?"

"Nell—I don't—we can't . . ." He shifted his weight from side to side, pulled on his chin, and rubbed the deep creases that had formed on his forehead. He looked down at his shoes and said, "I don't have the money. I thought about asking for an advance from the boss, to send you alone, but who would take care of the children? I have to work."

"My daddy, my daddy . . ." I turned my back on him, the children, the apartment, and stared at the window. There I found my fractured reflection.

"We'll have your momma come here to visit, soon as I can send her a ticket. It'll be good for her to see the grandbabies and you. And one day we'll all go back to visit the family. I'm so sorry about your daddy."

I saw Daddy's face again, remembered what he had said to me about holding my marriage gently, like an apple, and using the knife for good. I closed my eyes, rubbing my chest where I thought my heart should be, and quietly hummed a church hymn as I shuffled to the bed. Henry kissed me on the cheek and pulled the quilt over my shoulders. I lay on my side, staring at nothingness through the film of moisture covering my face, my cheek pressed against a piece of Momma's delicate lace. I began to smell the hogs again, the stink of a pen that needed cleaning.

But no, it was April's full, hot, steaming diaper. I could see Henry turning his face in disgust as he worked at cleaning her before putting on a new diaper. Junior was holding his nose, standing as far away as he could. Henry picked April up with his free arm and slowly walked to the toilet. Junior crept behind them, curious about how his daddy was going to do what he had only seen his momma do each day. *My family*, I thought, *here are my babies with their daddy.*

I reached for the letter and pressed it flat, smoothing all the wrinkles I had made from clenching it. I needed to touch Momma's words, to trace the letters she had made and let the weight of Daddy's death flow from my fingertips to my heart. She said they'd gotten all my letters and read them. But how? My family didn't read. How had she known what was in those letters? I had known as I wrote them that no one in the family could read well enough to go through each one easily. I'd promised to write, and so I did. I'd thought maybe my brothers might read the letters aloud, since they'd had some schooling. I'd used short sentences, small words, easy for anyone with simple reading skills to understand. But now I wanted to know.

"Henry? You said you talked to Momma."

"I told you, she called me at work."

"You heard my momma speak. Talked to her. Almost two years, and all I can do is imagine the sound of her voice in my ears. What did she say?"

"I told you, she . . ."

"I want to know every word she said, what her voice sounded like, what she said about the family. How long did you and she talk? What day? Did you just come home that day, eat, polish your shoes, like nothing was different? How is that possible?"

"Nell . . ."

"No! Tell me what I need to know."

"All right."

"Who read my letters to them?"

"Miss Parker," he said.

"What?"

"Your momma said that Miss Parker read your letters to everyone. She'd come by the house, sit on the front porch, and read your letters so that the whole family, and the neighbors, could hear what you wrote."

*Miss Parker*, I whispered to myself. *Reading my letters. Miss Parker!* "What'd you ask Momma about Miss Parker?"

"What do you mean?"

"I know there's been more between you two than you've said."

"I don't understand. We grew up together, that's all."

"That's not all!" I shouted. "Mention her name and you light up like a candle. Tell me she's *Mary*, not Miss Parker like I say. You care for her, don't you?"

"She's a friend. Our parents were close, and we spent

time together—as friends. You're just upset, confused. Believe me."

"No reason for me to believe you, not about anything. But I started out that way. Believed that being married to you, living in the North, would be a great adventure."

I went to the window, pulled the curtain back, and opened it just a crack. I could hear the chaotic street noises that I still hadn't gotten used to. Cars rushed by below as if everyone were headed to someplace very important. People honked their horns if another driver didn't immediately take off when the light changed from red to green. It'd be impossible to measure the time between the light changing and a car horn honking. Exhaust lingered in the air and floated up through the window. The thick burnt-oil smell caught in my nostrils.

I missed Louisiana smells, the cooking fat Momma used to prepare fried fish or chicken, sausage or eggs. You could see the fat in the air, watch it cling to the thin curtains in the kitchen until, once a year, Momma tackled the project of taking all the curtains down to scrub them in the wash basin out back. She'd assign each of us a section of the kitchen wall to clean, using white-vinegar-laced warm water and hard bristle brushes that were also used to brush our donkey. "Scrub until you can see a shine," she'd say. Momma would leave the room, and our scrubbing would turn into a game of throwing water at each other, trying to rub each other's arms, back, and legs. "I'm gonna make you shine," we taunted. Our bodies dripped with water, and small puddles formed on the floor by our feet. When Momma came back and saw the mess, she'd tell us, "The floor is next, so you children have a good start on that project." We'd scrurry back to our sections of wall, still pushing and shoving one another, our laughter muffled in our throats.

I turned away from the window, leaned my weight against the sill, and looked at our home. I couldn't wash the walls here. There was faded and peeling wallpaper everywhere. It had a large floral pattern that looked as if someone had tried to make the place seem grand and expensive. In truth, it was anything but grand. There was a brown water stain in the ceiling over the sink, and plaster hung in spots, just waiting for a good jolt from the unit above ours to come loose and land on the counter. The furniture had been here when we moved in. "Fully furnished," Henry had said as we walked up the three flights of stairs to our new home. Back then I'd seen a beautiful overstuffed chair with smart pillows, a charming folding table with mismatched wooden chairs that seemed to go nicely together, a double bed with four metal posts and a colorful quilt neatly folded at the foot.

Now I saw drab sleeping quarters that brought me more pain than comfort. The only good thing about the bed was my family quilt, made with my momma's hands. The kitchen occupied one wall of the apartment—a small metal sink; a counter just large enough to hold some pots and pans; an apartment-sized stove with two burners and an oven; a frayed, braided, oval rug in the middle of the room that must have been colorful at some time in its past but was dingy now; and one tall dresser with a mirror that had lost most of its ability to reflect a person's image. The door to the bathroom was directly across from the bed. I could roll over and see the toilet, listen to the dripping faucet in the bathtub. Since that first day we had added two children to our home and the many things that came with them—a crib, play-things, and diapers, so many diapers.

*Miss Parker*, I thought, *reading my letters*. She'd proba-bly helped Momma with the letter too, it was so well phrased. *Miss Parker*—I wouldn't want her to see this place.

I walked to the door, opened it, and stepped into the hallway. My feet carried me down the stairwell before my mind knew I was moving. I felt free, the way Josie had looked as she left the other day. The night air was crisp and cool on my face. I sat on the stoop, pulled my dress tight over my knees, rested my head, and let waves of sorrow take over. I talked to Daddy between sobs. "You told me I was meant to be something special. I let you down. I'm trying to be a good wife, but I'm not sure what that looks like. You and Momma made it seem so easy, as though you fit together, a matching set moving in tandem. I feel invisible, lurking in the spaces of other peoples' lives. I want to be better, be the person you believed in. Miss you. Love you."

My family was waiting upstairs. I wandered back and watched them. April was sleeping, and Junior was quietly playing at his daddy's feet with a small ball that he kept kicking and then running after. Henry's eyelids were getting heavy as he relaxed on the edge of the bed. He looked like one of the children, fighting off sleep in fear of missing some action in the room.

"Henry," I said, "I'm going home to see Momma."

He rubbed his forehead, dragged his hand over his eyes and down his nose, and began rubbing his neck, working out a kink that had settled there. Finally he shook his head and stared at the floor. "Nell, I know you want to see Momma, but I can't afford it."

"I can buy the bus tickets."

"With what?"

"I have my own money."

Henry stood and walked toward me, a worried look on his face. "How's that?" He gave me a sideways stare, making me feel the way I always had when Momma caught me doing something she'd said not to.

"I worked for Ginny—did her books, handled the phones. She paid me for my time, told me the money would come in handy one day. That day is here." My shoulders were back, my chin firm, my eyes fixed on his.

The blood vessels in Henry's neck began to bulge, as though air were running through his veins. His nose flared like a hog's, angry and mean. He took another step toward me, never wavering in his intense gaze. "Those damn women, they twisted your mind all upside-down. You had no business being with them. I never gave you permission to work."

"I don't need your permission. And your son wouldn't be here if it hadn't been for Ginny and Mabel. Without them I'd have died alone in labor. They're the reason I have any mind left at all, what with being locked in this minuscule world— no phone, no television, no adult conversation, my family so far away!"

"Huh! And you call me a liar, you say you can't believe me? What about you?" He took a step back, grabbed his jacket, and rushed out the door.

Henry came home late that night. The children were asleep, and I was curled in a knot; sleep wouldn't come. I heard him open the door, trying to be quiet and not wake us. I stayed in my fetal position, eyes pressed shut. Henry didn't touch me when he got into bed. I didn't touch him either.

In the morning he crept out of bed much earlier than usual, got ready for work, and left. I pretended to be asleep. When I put my feet on the floor to greet the day, I noticed something on the table—bus tickets for Louisiana.

## Chapter Thirteen

WE ARRIVED AT THE BUS STATION IN LOUISIANA ON Saturday morning. I collected our suitcase and turned to see our old truck parked in nearly the same spot it had been on the day I said good-bye to the farm. I could see my daddy standing beside the truck, his hand raised, signaling hello, looking just as he had some two years ago when he waved farewell. The glare of the sun made me faint; it was only as I shaded my eyes that I saw it was my oldest brother Robert by the pick-up. He stood just as tall and straight, the large muscles in his arms pressing against the torn sleeves of his T-shirt.

"Hi, Sis," he said as I approached. "Welcome home." He bent down and gave me a tender hug. I couldn't remember ever being hugged by Robert. He was at least ten years older than I was—a quiet man like Daddy. He had always been at Daddy's side—working the fields, repairing the house, making sure the truck and all the farm equipment ran properly. He'd sit on the porch with Daddy and the other men, chatting about the day's work and neighborhood events.

"I thought you were Daddy."

"I know. I miss him too." He picked up Junior and held him over his head. "Hello, little man. I'm your Uncle Bobby."

Junior looked scared at first, a frown developing in the corners of his mouth, but Robert kept bouncing him until peals of laughter emitted from Junior's belly. He kicked his legs in the air and spread his arms as if he were taking flight into the clouds.

"This here's April," I said, holding her up to Robert so she could meet her uncle too. April drooled and held out her arms. Her right hand made a hello wave as she opened and closed her fingers.

Robert put Junior down and took April from my arms. She immediately patted her hand all over his face, examining the new territory. Satisfied that she was safe with him, she rested her head on his shoulder and began sucking her thumb. The four of us stood at the side of the truck, locked in a tight hug, Junior clinging to Robert's trouser leg. I took in the smell of Robert, the rich soil caked in the creases of his neck. Tears began to sting my eyes.

He had been first to bring a wife home—Bernice—when she was just sixteen. I'd thought she would be a playmate for me, even though she was older. Instead she became my babysitter and Momma's helper. They had never had any babies of their own. Once I'd spied Bernice and Momma in the kitchen. She and Robert had been married over a year by then. Bernice was crying, "I don't know what's wrong with me." Momma had rubbed her back, saying, "Sometimes it's just not meant to be. You and Robert should pray on it."

Bernice became the aunt who cared for all the other babies that arrived as each brother married and his wife moved into the house. She was neither angry nor sad, simply joyful to have so many children around her, so many beings she could care for and love. She called them all her babies.

Robert was a loving uncle, teased and played with the kids, taught the boys how to fish and cut wood, held the girls' hands and let them ride on his shoulders so they could see the whole world from up high. Sometimes, though, he got a sad look as he watched the growing gaggle of children run from him to their parents' arms, the arms of his younger brothers, for comfort.

"How is Momma?" I asked as we began to drive home.

"Sad," he said, without taking his eyes off the road. "He'd gotten so weak before . . ."

"I can't imagine Daddy being weak," I sighed.

"He couldn't get out of bed. Momma had to feed him. I took over the farm."

"Did he suffer?"

I touched the open compartment on the dashboard. Stuff was strewn about just as I remembered. Once I'd asked Daddy what it all was. He'd told me there were important things— the registration for the truck in case he got stopped and accused of stealing it; shopping lists of things he needed for the farm and Momma needed for the kitchen; a tire gauge to check the air; an old picture of him and Momma when they were much younger; a picture of all of us from Christmas time when I was just a baby; a small prayer book from church; and some candy "just for you." I'd unwrapped the candy and quickly forgotten about the other items.

Now I imagined the taste of the sweet, gooey caramel sticking to my teeth as I heard Robert say, "Yes, he couldn't use his own body the way he wanted to. He was suffering. Didn't make a sound in complaint—just did what he could, accepted what we could do for him. I was on one side, Momma on the other. At the end he looked up at us and was gone, just gone." Robert turned his face away from me and wiped his eyes.

My heart was pounding against my chest so hard I was certain that Robert could see and hear it. "I'm sorry I wasn't here."

"Nothing you could've done. You were where you needed to be."

We rode in a heavy silence for a while. Finally Robert said, "Sis, your children are beautiful."

"Thank you. They're a blessing."

"Bernice is going to love them."

I took his hand. "I can't wait for them to meet her, Momma, the whole family."

Clouds of dust floated around us as the truck bounced down the old unpaved road. I rested my arm on the open window. Grit began to stick to my skin; the humid early-summer air kissed my eyelashes. It felt as though there were parallel universes looming before me. The past familiarity— open fields, cotton and corn plants dotting the landscape, pecan trees sprouting tender fruit, cows and mules eating contentedly—all belonged in one universe. But the space in the truck between me and Robert—him sitting in the grooves created by years of Daddy's frame pressed into the fabric, me occupying the indentations that had belonged to Robert, and the empty middle space where I'd always sat wedged between the two of them—that was the present world tugging at my soul. I wanted to dream reality away— my life with Henry up North, the emptiness of the front seat, even the children fidgeting behind us.

April's cries snapped me out of my reverie.

"Can we stop at the general store? I need to get more

diapers for April. I bet it all looks the same, the store and all."

"It does, Sis. Nothing much has changed here. Same old man runs the place, same old people hanging around just to snoop on everyone else. Nothing's changed except that I go there now, instead of Daddy."

I continued to stroke Robert's hand as I stared out the side window.

We pulled up to the general store, and the old sensibility gripped me again. Often church ladies would talk about having an out-of-body experience, where you felt as though you were hovering above looking down at yourself, watching. I felt that way looking at the store. I could see the younger me walking with Daddy up the steps, him telling me to be quiet and stay close by his side, me examining the sweets, deciding which candies I'd take home, Daddy waiting patiently as the whites were tended to, keeping his head down as he paid for the goods, gently guiding me out the door before I questioned him about anything.

"I'll be just a minute," I said to Robert as I opened the car door.

"Here," Robert said as he handed me a ten-dollar bill. "Just in case you need it."

Henry had left a little cash for me with the bus tickets. I hadn't needed much. Whenever the bus had stopped, I'd bought something for us to drink, but otherwise I'd carried enough food to last us the long ride. I never counted the money, before we left or after I spent any of it. I didn't know how much diapers would cost here.

"Thank you." I stepped out of the car to make my way into the store.

"Be careful, Sis—this is the same South."

April and Junior were fast asleep in the back seat. I smoothed my dress as best as I could, adjusted my hat so it sat straight on my head, placed my purse on my arm at the elbow, and held my gloved hand at a relaxed angle, just dangling from my wrist. With my chin held high I took a first step toward the front door.

The red coca-cola cooler was still to the right of the door, just as I remembered. I could almost taste the cold dark fizz flowing down my throat as my lips circled the green-tinted bottle. It had always been a treat to have Daddy get us our own bottles of soda pop to hold and sip as we waited outside for him. Momma had never liked for us to have soda-pop. *It'll ruin your teeth. You children should only have milk and water.* I could hear her reprimand whenever she caught Daddy letting us have a coke. *They'll be okay,* Daddy'd say, just as we finished the last gulp.

To the left of the door, a few steps away, was the one gas pump for miles around. The red star and circle of the Texaco sign didn't look as bright as I remembered. There was a dullness to it, as though it had been battered by strong winds. The pock marks denting the once-smooth surface had likely been made by kids taking aim with small rocks. The pungent scent of gasoline, hanging heavy in the dusty air, clung to the tiny hairs in my nostrils. I stood still and took deep breaths, as though smelling the sweet fragrance of freshly bloomed roses.

Robert leaned toward the passenger side window. "Sis, you okay?"

"I'm just enjoying being home."

I walked up the last few steps and pulled open the

creaking screen door, its holes so large the bugs had no trouble getting inside.

As I entered the old man said, "Morn'n," without looking up at me.

I replied, "Good morning. I need some diapers for my little one."

"Right down the end there, in the back, you'll find plenty."

He still hadn't made eye contact with me. Not that it was intentional; he was busy marking prices on some dishes stacked on the counter by the cash register. I recognized him, the owner, the white man who had embarrassed my daddy.

I brought the diapers to the counter. Only then did he look up, and a glimmer of recognition came across his face. "You Jones's daughter, the one done moved up yonder." It wasn't a question but a statement of common knowledge. Probably the neighbors had sat around the store and talked about the young girl who had left home to travel North as a child bride.

"Yes, *Mr. Jones* was my daddy."

"Good man. Sorry 'bout your loss."

His comment fell on my heart like a sharp knife, causing me to wince in pain. I gritted my teeth, took a deep breath, and was about to scowl at him and say, "You called my daddy *boy*, made him leave your store." But Robert's words of caution rang in the back of my mind. I thought about my children, innocently waiting in the back seat of the truck; about Robert, who was already concerned that I might have forgotten how to behave; about Momma at the farm, her heart in mourning for Daddy—she didn't need any problem caused by my sassing this white man. So I said, "I remember coming here with Daddy after that boy was killed in Mississippi. My daddy was uncomfortable, almost scared. I didn't like seeing him that way."

I steeled my chin, expecting him to lash back at me. Instead he looked almost sad and held my gaze for a moment longer than was needed. He spoke in a whisper, looking from side to side to make certain no one else was around. "Sometimes you have to do things that don't always agree with the heart. You up yonder now, probably think our ways here are bad and mean. You've seen how it can be different. Your daddy was a good man. He and I understood each other. He knew when I didn't have a choice about things."

"He was my *daddy*." My eyes began to sting from tears I didn't want to fall down my cheeks.

"Things can't always be the way you want it. Grown-ups know this. Time you understood it too." He looked away and rang up my purchase of diapers. It came to nine dollars and fifty cents. Just as I handed him the ten-dollar bill Robert had given me, a white family entered the store. They stopped, apparently waiting for me to step aside so their needs could be taken care of before mine.

"Here," he said to me. The tone of his voice had changed from kindly to that of a white shop-owner bothered by this colored woman taking up space in his shop. "Your change. Now move along."

He handed me back the ten-dollar bill that I had given to him. For a moment his fingers were on one end of the money and mine on the other.

"You got your stuff. Now take your change and leave." He shooed me away with his arm while asking the couple if he could help them.

I took the bill, fumbled with my purse, and slipped it inside. Then I turned and faced the couple behind me. For a quick moment I looked the woman straight in the eye. She was about to say something when I lowered my gaze, staring at the tips of my shoes—shoes that needed to be polished. I backed away to the door. Behind me I heard the other man ask, "That colored girl giving you any trouble?"

The old man replied, "No, she's the Jones girl. Lost her daddy. Back visiting from the North. Think she forgot this here is the South. I put her back in her place. Now what do you fine people need?"

The top step came at my feet before I realized it, causing me to stumble and lose my balance. I almost bumped into the truck, so resolute was my downcast gaze. I put the package of diapers on the floor in the back and made my way into the front seat. With trembling hands, racing heart, a tight knot tugging at my stomach, I sat and handed Robert his ten dollars.

"Had enough money of your own?"

"Guess I did, thanks just the same."

"Sis, you okay? Something happen in there?"

"Nothing happened. I just remembered what I'd forgotten about here."

April and Junior were still asleep, huddled next to each other in the baby seats Robert had strapped into the back. I ran my hand over their cheeks and hair. *My babies are Northern children*, I thought. *I don't want them to grow up afraid of a white accusing finger thrust their way, robbing them of innocence and possibly their lives.* I moved my hand back and forth on my stomach, while taking in the beauty of our surroundings.

After a time Robert asked, "What's it like up North, Sis? Is it as different as everyone says? Are we free there?"

*Free?* I saw an image of my life, always confined to our tiny apartment, with two children, never going out on my own, no money in my pockets, waiting for Henry to come home and lead us out into the world. *Free?*

"I guess we are. There aren't any signs saying we can't go somewhere or shop or drink water." My voice trailed off.

"How's your church?" he asked.

"Church?"

"You do go to church, don't you?"

"Henry goes. I always have a Sunday dinner ready when he comes home. He tells me about the sermon and the hymns. He has some favorite hymns he'll hum for us. Little Junior is beginning to learn them and can hum along with his daddy. I know most of the hymns from our church here. I could sing all of them, but I don't. Henry likes to hum." I was fiddling with my dress and looking at my lap. I reflected on how Henry would leave me at home, at first alone and then with the children. He'd told me in the early months, "You're too delicate to walk all the way to church. Just stay here and have a nice Sunday dinner ready when I return; then I'll read some of the bible to you." As if I needed him to read to me. I was a reader. Henry struggled with words and sentences like the school kids in Miss Parker's class. Whenever he heard me reading aloud, he'd tell me, "Hush, you're making too much noise." Once I'd started to have babies, Sunday would come around and Henry'd say, "The children are too young to be in church. You need to stay home with them. I'll tell you everything the minister preaches." And off he'd go. I couldn't bear to share this with Robert.

"Sis, have the children been christened?"

"Christened? I—we—never thought about it. I just do what Henry wants, what he needs. Now I do whatever he and the children need. I don't think about things like church and such. I don't think much anymore." I shook my head as though I was trying to air out a room where dust had filled every corner.

"You were always the thinker at home, Sis. The one person who had to know how everything worked. You wore Daddy and Momma out. Daddy used to joke that you would take the truck apart if you could, just to look at the insides. You knew more about the world than any of us. I know you and I didn't talk much, and I was too old to play or hang out with you, but I thought you were the smartest girl around. I was proud of my little sis. Still am. You'll figure out how to make things work at your home; it takes time. Look, you got married, moved up yonder, have two babies and a new world to figure out, and now we're mourning for our daddy. It's a lot for anyone."

"I guess." Suddenly I felt like a little girl again, confused about the world around me. I wanted to ask Robert so many questions. I just didn't know the right ones to ask. As for the smart and inquisitive girl, I couldn't remember her. *What happened to that girl?* I took deep breaths to ease the upside-down feeling that had a grip on me.

"I think you need to prepare yourself to see Momma. She's not doing well."

"She's not sick too?"

"In a way. She's sad about Daddy, of course, but there's something else."

"Robert, what is it?"

"I can't really say. She seems lost. Bernice has taken over for Momma at the house, the way I took over for Daddy on the farm. We never thought our lives would turn out this way. I thought we'd eventually get a place of our own, raise children; but here we are. Anyway, I wanted to let you know before you saw her."

I squeezed his hand.

The front porch was empty when Robert pulled into the dusty driveway of our farmhouse. I stared at the worn front steps, the crooked siding that was peeling more than I remembered; everything had been battered by wind and time.

The children were wide awake, hungry, dirty, and ready for clean diapers.

"Sis, I'll take care of the children. You go ahead and find Momma."

I stood at the base of the porch, wanting to walk right up and into the house, but my feet wouldn't move. Daddy's rocking chair was creaking back and forth as if he were sitting there, talking to the other men on a lazy summer evening. I could hear his voice, that deep baritone sound coming from the base of his belly. His laughter rang in my ears, and I doubled over, grabbing my stomach to ease the pain.

Around the back of the house I found Momma. She was bent over the wash bucket scrubbing sheets and clothes, moving her hands on the metal scrub-board that rested inside the bucket. She was humming a church hymn as her hands moved up and down in the hard water, beating every germ out of the sheets. "A good clean is important," she used to tell me when she'd taught me how to clean linens years ago. "It hurts, Momma," I'd protest, hoping my complaints would free me from the chore, but it never worked. "Sometimes good things hurt," she'd said, and piled on more items for me to wash and hang on the line.

I moved to the wash bucket, began to hum along with Momma, and put my hands in the wash to help her. She looked up at me, her hands never stopping their dance on the scrub-board. "Welcome home, Baby Girl."

Up and down, up and down, our bodies swayed in rhythm as the clothes slid in and out of the soapy water. It was as though we were on a seesaw, two children enjoying the warm day. Sheets and pillowcases on the clothes-line moved back and forth in harmony with us; at times they fluttered across Momma's face like white sails kissing the wind. Sudsy water climbed up to my elbows. My skin welcomed the mingling of moisture and outside air, as it used to when I was a Southern child living in open spaces.

Momma's humming turned into singing:

*On a hill far away stood an old rugged cross,*
*The emblem of suff'ring and shame,*
*And I love that old cross where the Dearest and Best*
*For a world of lost sinners was slain.*

I responded with the second stanza:

*So I'll cherish the old rugged cross,*
*Till my trophies at last I lay down;*
*I will cling to the old rugged cross,*
*And exchange it some day for a crown.*

We sang the final stanzas together:

*Oh, that old rugged cross, so despised by the world*
*Has a wondrous attraction for me;*
*For the dear Lamb of God left His glory above,*
*To bear it to dark Calvary.*

*In the old rugged cross, stained with blood so divine,*
*A wondrous beauty I see;*
*For 'twas on that old cross Jesus suffered and died,*
*To pardon and sanctify me.*

"You remember that hymn? My favorite."

"I remember. You always sang it whenever you braided my hair. I'd sit between your legs, and you'd tug at me to keep still and sing along with you. It was the only way I could forget about the pain of your fingers pulling at my tight hair."

Momma was wearing the black and red checked house-dress that I hadn't seen in two years. It looked exactly the same except for a cluster of dark stains below her chest and a torn patch dangling at the sleeve. Small white buttons danced down the front of the frock, all the way to the hem-line that rested just below her knees. A matching belt was tied off-center in a bow at her waist to keep the ends out of the way while she washed and cleaned. I could see the edge of a lace hankie tucked into her side pocket; it looked as if she needed a clean dry one.

I slid my hand on top of hers and inched closer to her side. Our hands came out of the water on the same piece of clothing. At first I thought it was one of Robert's T-shirts, but as the light hit it, the embroidered letter *D* on the right sleeve began to take shape. When my brothers had grown to nearly the size of Daddy, we'd stitched the first letter of their names on the shirts so everyone would know which were theirs. *D* was for Daddy. I reached into the water and pulled out another; the *D* was there too. The same was true with each one I grabbed. The long-sleeved white dress shirt didn't have an initial on it, but I recognized it as the one Daddy had worn to church every Sunday.

I backed away from the bucket. "Momma! These are Daddy's."

"Shush, Baby Girl. Your daddy expects me to have all his clothes clean and pressed. That's what I do. That's what I'll continue to do. Keep washing. Tell me, do you sing these hymns in your church?"

"Hymns are the same everywhere." I stared deep into the suds-filled water and saw the image of Henry's back as he walked out of the apartment for church on Sundays.

"Have my grandbabies been christened? No mention of that in your letters."

"They're young yet. In time."

Momma stopped. I could feel her fixed look on me. Her eyes, full of sorrow, bore into my skin, causing a burning sensation to rise up into my cheeks. I raised my eyes to hers, but I didn't say anything as she continued scrutinizing me, searching for an answer to her question, the right answer. When she couldn't see it, she shook her head in disappointment and said, "Your daddy left something for you. Go on up to the porch. On his chair. You'll see it. Go on now. I'll finish here."

"Yes, Momma." I dropped my eyes, wiped my hands on my dress, and backed away.

The worn front steps, which were in dire need of sweeping, creaked as I slowly moved to Daddy's rocking chair. There I saw a small box I hadn't noticed earlier. It was rough-hewn, made from the wood Daddy used to whittle stick figures and smoking pipes. Its lid was cut precisely to fit into the grooves on the sides of the top, so you could slide it out to reveal treasures inside. Daddy had taken pride in creating wooden things that served a purpose and didn't need any screws or nails to make them work. There were etchings on the top of the box that spelled *Baby Girl*. I gently held Daddy's gift and rubbed my fingers over the letters. It felt as though his large calloused hands were guiding me.

"This here is how you cut the letters into the wood."

"Am I doing it right, Daddy?"

"Yes, Baby Girl. You got it. You have a way with this knife."

"I can carve, just like you, can't I, Daddy?"

"Yes, Baby Girl, you sure know how to handle my knife."

"Sis," Robert said before I opened the box. "Did you see Momma?" He walked onto the porch, cleaning his hands of the grease from a piece of farm equipment he'd been working on.

"She doesn't look well, Robert. At first I thought she looked exactly the same as when I'd last seen her. But then I saw the stains and tears on her dress, the deep dark circles under her eyes, the red lines around her irises. There was a faraway aspect to her gaze, as though she didn't really see me or know where she was. And I was helping her wash but then realized it's Daddy's things she's scrubbing clean, like he's still here."

"She's been that way since he died. She just floats around the house and out back, doing chores with the aim of pleasing Daddy. I hear her talking to him all the time; I've even heard her get into an argument with herself, believing it was him not agreeing with her. We're worried—it seems to be getting worse each day. We don't leave her alone; we're not sure what'll happen in the kitchen if she's on her own."

*Momma*, I thought as I rocked in Daddy's chair, clutching my box, *and here I was hoping you could ease my pain.* "Maybe I should stay. She needs me."

"You have a home. What about Henry?"

"Wouldn't miss me."

He sat next to me in the chair Momma used to sit in to be close to Daddy. "Sis, is everything all right with you and Henry? We all noticed that you never mention him in your letters."

"Remember the adventures in my books I'd talk about? I thought that getting married and moving North would be my personal adventure; that I'd be out in the world meeting people, doing interesting things, dressed in fine clothes. Instead I sit in a cramped apartment all day with two babies, waiting for Henry to come home so I can take care of his needs. That isn't what I wanted."

"Your children are beautiful, a real blessing. Bernice and me would give anything to have babies of our own. You should be grateful."

"Please don't get me wrong. I love my children, it's just that . . . I wanted more than Henry wanting me all the time. That's all."

"He's your husband."

"Don't mean I have to like it." I listened to the creak of the rocking chair scrape against the old porch slats, rubbing Daddy's gift box in my hands. I imagined if I rubbed hard enough, I might be able to will a genie out of the box who would grant me three wishes.

"How's that library job you wrote about?" Robert asked.

"Don't go there anymore. Henry didn't like me being out. Don't go to the hairdresser any longer either; but at least I'm allowed to have the girls visit me one day a week. I miss the library. There was a group of young children I read to. One of the little girls reminded me of who I used to be."

Robert patted the top of my head as he stood and said, "Well, I'd better get back to that tractor, finish with it before supper. Nell, spend time with Momma, but then you need to go home to your husband—that's where you belong. Even if there're things you need to work on. Bernice and me will take care of Momma." He lumbered to the barn, his shoulders angled down as if big hands were pressing against him. He probably thought he couldn't offer me empathy where Henry was concerned; that was a woman's matter.

I watched him disappear inside the barn and found comfort in the back-and-forth motion of Daddy's rocking chair. The expanse of early fall air enveloped my skin in welcome memories of a past life full of anticipation. But I could hear Junior and April inside with Bernice, who I hadn't even said hello to yet. Their voices grounded me in my present reality.

Momma walked up to the porch, drying her hands on the front of her apron, and said, "Baby Girl, did you find the gift from Daddy?"

"Yes, ma'am."

"Did you open the box?"

"Not yet. Robert and I got to talking, and I just wanted to feel it in my hands. Made me think about Daddy."

She sat in her chair with a heavy sigh, looked straight

out, and began to rock slowly back and forth. I noticed patches of gray in her hair, sticking out like wires with a mind of their own. Deep wrinkles danced at the corners of her eyes and the sides of her lips. She held no expression on her face, it was like an image caught in a picture, similar to the one of my grandparents hanging on the wall.

"Momma, are you all right?" I placed my hand on top of hers. She pulled away.

"Seems everyone thinks I'm madder than a wet hen these days. I can see it in their eyes, the way Robert, Bernice, and the others tiptoe around me, always whispering to each other. Y'all may have lost your daddy, and that's real sad. But I lost *half* of me. Everything about my life was wrapped up in your daddy. I woke each morning thinking about what I needed to do as one half of the whole that he and I were. If his right leg moved forward, my left leg followed; if he reached with his left hand, my right hand instantly connected to his. We danced every day to the same rhythm—raising all of you, working this farm, solving problems, dealing with the white man—without having to say a word to each other. My body's been cut down the middle. Is it any wonder I'm out of sorts?"

"Momma."

"Enough about me. What about you, Baby Girl? Why're you hollow inside?"

"I'm sad about Daddy, not being here to say a proper good-bye."

"My guess—that hollowness been growing for a long time. I can see that the bright spark of curiosity and love of life that lit up those eyes was been dim well before Daddy passed. Almost two years, over twenty letters, and not one mention of your husband. Why aren't you happy with Henry?"

I squirmed in the chair, began to rock faster back and forth, squeezed the box so tightly that the edges left deep marks in my hands. "I'm not half of a whole, like you and Daddy. It's more like I'm a fixture, a piece of furniture even, little more than a slave doing the master's bidding, having his babies. I didn't want babies this soon; he knew it, but he just keeps taking me."

Momma spun toward me and grabbed my chin. "Look at me! Don't you ever say you don't want your babies! You're *my* last child. If I ever spoke those words—didn't want a baby this late in life—it'd be you I'd be talking about! Understand?"

"Yes, ma'am."

"Does he hurt you?"

"No, ma'am."

"Do you love him?"

"I don't know."

"Does he love you?"

"I guess, in his way."

"Do you sass him?"

"No!"

"Why not?"

"What?"

"Baby Girl I knew, sassed all the time. What happened to her?"

"Don't know. Maybe she just got swallowed up in the distance from this farm to the arms of loneliness up yonder. But maybe I should stay here."

"No! You and your children belong at home with their daddy."

"That's what Robert said."

"He's right. Now I'm gonna help Bernice with supper, be the *crazy* woman so they can know I need them. What I'm really doing is searching for the right pieces to quilt my life back together with—the way you need to."

I grabbed Momma's waist and buried my face in her bosom. My nostrils filled with the scent of washing detergent, cooking grease, and farm animals that clung to the fabric of her dress. Her breasts were as soft and comforting as I'd remembered, but her bones were more prominent, almost as if sharp edges were against my arms.

She tilted my face to hers, wiped the tears on my cheeks with her thumbs, and said, "You the strongest child ever. Daddy and I both knew that. Find yourself. That's where you'll discover your happiness."

"How, Momma?"

"Pray on it. You do remember how to pray?"

"Yes, ma'am."

She squeezed me to her chest. "I love you, Baby Girl; your daddy loves you. When you open Daddy's box, remember what he said about marriage."

Then she went inside. I could hear the children's excited squeals when Bernice told them, "This is your grams." I looked at my last gift from Daddy that was still nestled in my hand. The top easily slid open. Inside was Daddy's whittling knife.

BERNICE RANG THE dinner bell, and the family made its way to the dining-room table. Momma, Robert, and the others each passed Daddy's chair and touched it ever so gently, as though it were fragile, like a tender egg. I stood behind his chair a moment and caressed the worn wood imprinted with the impression of Daddy's back. We sat in our respective places at the table, me in the same chair I had occupied until the day I became a bride. Momma took her place beside Daddy's spot, where the red and white checkered napkin he always used was resting on the plate. His favorite drinking glass, an old green-tinted mason jar with a piece of metal encircling the rim and connected to a bent handle, was to the right of the plate.

We held hands and bowed our heads for prayer. But rather than a prayer of thanks, Momma said, "Robert, time for you to move to the head of the table."

"Momma?" Robert asked.

"It's time. You the man of this household now. Take your rightful place."

Robert slowly rose, eyed each of us as though seeking agreement or permission, and made his way to Daddy's chair. As he pulled the chair away from the table, the legs made a screeching sound. We gasped. Robert froze, looked around the table and then at Momma. She nodded, and he sat down.

"Children," Momma said, "I know y'all are worried about me. No need for that. We each have to come to terms with losing Daddy in our own way. Mine is to do the things that bring me comfort—washing his clothes, holding his rocking chair as though my hand is resting on his, speaking to him like his breath is tickling the side of my ear, stroking his hair brush to take in the scent of him. It may seem like I've drifted far away, I haven't. This is my way of finding the contours of my new nest filled with memories. It's a comfort to have Baby Girl home. Although she'll only be here a short time, we can all begin to heal together. Tomorrow we'll visit Daddy's grave as a family and say a proper good-bye; he would want that. Now, Robert, say grace."

We held hands and lowered our heads as Robert spoke the prayer that Daddy had always shared.

WE FORMED A small procession in the morning. Momma led, holding onto Robert's arm. Bernice and I followed them. Everyone else fell behind us, paired in twos, with the children at the end tended by my younger brothers. The family plot rested at the furthest point of the farm, away from the animals and house but close enough to be visible from the front porch, especially when the sun set behind the lone tree that shaded the area. We made our way up the natural, uneven footpath that had been cut through the weeds over the years. Every Sunday after my grandparents passed away, Daddy had made his way to their graves to say a prayer. Sometimes Momma had joined him. Sometimes I had. But he had mostly gone alone just before church, when he was dressed in his Sunday best. I'd once asked Momma why her parents weren't buried here. "They're at my family's plot, back where I grew up," she'd said. "Why don't you visit their burial site, the way Daddy does?" I'd asked then. She never answered.

We formed a circle around Daddy's grave. Momma handed me the family bible she had been clutching. I took it and read marked passages from Ecclesiastes 3:

*To every thing there is a season, and a time to*
*every purpose under the heaven:*
*A time to be born, and a time to die; a time to*
*plant, and a time to pluck up that which is planted;*
*A time to weep, and a time to laugh; a time to*
*mourn, and a time to dance;*
*A time to cast away stones, and a time to gather*
*stones together; a time to embrace, and a time to*
*refrain from embracing;*
*A time to get, and a time to lose; a time to keep,*
*and a time to cast away;*
*A time to rend, and a time to sew; a time to keep*
*silence, and a time to speak;*
*A time to love, and a time to hate; a time of war,*
*and a time of peace.*
*All go unto one place; all are of the dust, and all*
*turn to dust again . . .*

Momma knelt on the soil that was soft from gentle morning rain. She prayed silently while we huddled closer to one another, seeking solace from the warmth of our collective loss and love. When she was finished, Robert helped her up. We formed a closed circle with Momma in the center.

After a moment she pulled away and said, "It's time for you each to say good-bye. Then we'll go home as a newly shaped family and begin anew." She turned and walked away down the footpath towards the house.

Robert looked at me and nodded. I shook my head and backed away, gripped the bible to my chest, fought down the floating-feather-like feeling that was billowing inside of me, choking my throat. One by one, he and the others knelt to say their good-byes. I watched through tears streaming down my face. When the prayers were done, Robert touched my shoulder and said, "Sis, are you all right?"

"I need to be alone."

As he led the family away, I stepped closer to Daddy's grave and fell to my knees. My body rocked from side to side in spasms. I wanted to howl at the sky, but nothingness flowed from my heart and out my mouth.

I don't know how long I stayed at Daddy's side, whether I fainted or just lapsed into a deep sleep on the ground with my fingers grasping at dirt. All I can remember is Robert walking me back to the house and placing me on my bed.

## Chapter Fourteen

THE ONE-ROOM SCHOOLHOUSE SEEMED TO RISE UP out of the horizon like a misty figure coming into focus in a desert wind storm, a solitary oasis. My pace quickened with each step on the dusty road, as the place that had once been the center of my universe grew closer. However, I found myself torn between the excitement of returning to this sanctuary to find myself and the unfamiliar smallness and loneliness of the structure.

I walked slowly up to the door and watched Miss Parker at her desk. A terrible thirst seemed to grab hold of my throat, as if I needed a soothing cool drink to quench my parched body. I wanted to reach out to her, throw my arms around her waist, and ask if I could please come back, be her student like before.

"Nell!" Miss Parker said. "It's so good to see you." She rose and rushed to greet me. "I'm sorry about your daddy."

"I wanted to see you and thank you for reading my letters to the family. It was good of you."

"Hush. Of course I'd do that. Come now and visit with me."

We sat sideways in desk chairs, facing one another. I ran my fingertips over carved etchings of initials inside a misshaped heart with an arrow running through it. For a moment, time rewound in my mind. It was two years ago, and I was back in the rhythmic patterns of the end of the school day with Miss Parker. Daddy was home, cleaning up after a day of farm work, and Momma was preparing dinner for the night. I was free to spend time in school and then make my way through the grasses and trees of the surrounding fields to the safety and comfort of my home.

"Nell?"

"Sorry—I was drifting back to another time. I went to Daddy's grave yesterday. Now that I'm home, Momma wanted the family to say good-bye together. My wedding day was the last time he and I spoke, the last time he hugged me, kissed my forehead as he gave me away to Henry. I should've been here for him and Momma. There's this awful pain in my gut, Miss Parker. It's as though a ravenous hole is growing inside of me, as fast as a weed, and there's no way to fill it up."

"You're a good daughter—always remember that. Your daddy was proud of you. When one of your letters arrived, he'd call a gathering of the family, all the neighbors, and tell everyone to listen to your words. He loved your descriptions of life up North, how different it was from the surroundings here. But he liked it most when you wrote about how you missed the beauty of the farm, the smells of the animals, and the feel of wide open spaces that we here take for granted every day. Sometimes, as I read the letters, it looked as though your daddy's heart was gonna burst right through his chest."

My head dropped onto the desk as sorrow had its way with me. Miss Parker gently touched my arm but didn't make a sound. She let the waves of grief run through me. Once my body was spent, the heaving subsided, and my eyes gave up the relentless pursuit of tears, I raised my head and asked, "Does it go away, the pain?"

"It'll hurt for a time, but at some point you'll begin to fill up with memories of him that will warm you and bring comfort. You'll find yourself talking to him and actually believing he's responding. You'll think about him when you look at your own children and realize that now it's your job to be to them what he has been to you. His presence will always be there; it will ease the pain."

"How long did it take for you, after losing your daddy?"

"You recall how my father died. Well, the pain of how he was taken from us has never left me. I'll always hear my mother's howls, the men's deadly shouts, and my daddy telling Momma to go back inside and look after me. And his screams—too awful. It was so unnatural and yet sadly common. My pain endures. It'll be different for you. Your daddy lived a good life and was rewarded for his hard work with a loving family and close friends. It's never easy to lose a parent, but you have positive memories you can hold onto.

"Let me get you some water, and you can tell me about your adventures up North. It sounds like you've made a good life in Boston."

She made her way to the little sink, took a clean glass from the shelf positioned above, let the tap run to flush out brown stains, and allowed cool water into the glass. She handed me the glass and waited for me to take a sip. I could feel her eyes searching my face.

"Not sure what to say. I guess we've made a life, but it can be hard. Lonely. It's so unlike here. Coming back home, I suddenly realized how much I miss my family, the people, all the things I know."

"Takes time to get settled. It'll come. I remember how I felt when I went North. I had family who took me in, so that helped. But still I missed everything about being here—open spaces, the night sky so dark the stars sparkle, clean air, church services that lifted my spirits with song and prayer, even the sweltering heat of summer. I learned to like it there. It was more sophisticated. But I came back for my momma. She needed me. And then I lost her, but decided this was still where I should be. So I stayed."

A stillness fell over us. I looked around the room, taking in the smell of chalk from the blackboards, the faint aroma of ink still lingering in the wells at the desks for older students. I could almost see a ghost of myself at the desk I'd called my own for so many long days.

A young girl had come in to clean the room, just as I'd once done. Now she looked over at me with a worried expression on her face and stopped her cleaning. It was as if she felt guilty for being there.

I fiddled with the cross dangling from my neck. Miss Parker put her hand on mine and said, "Nell, what is it?"

"I need to ask you something. I've been carrying this in my belly since before my wedding. It keeps growing, like another baby that needs to come out but never seems quite ready." I looked her in the eye. "You and Henry, you grew up together. Did you two know each other—in a special way?"

Miss Parker looked over her shoulder and spoke to the young girl. "Dear, you can go now. You did a great job. Thank you."

The girl put the cleaning things away in the cabinet,

washed her hands in the sink in the corner of the room, and gathered up her belongings. She hurried past us toward the exit, stealing a quick glance at my face and saying, "Sorry 'bout your daddy" before she sped away.

"It was such a long time ago, Nell. We grew up together, Henry and me. Used to play down by the creek, run and chase each other like children do. Our families were close. Unlike most people around these parts, we were only children. I think that's why our parents spent so much time together. It made it seem like there were more of us around the table. Henry and I were inseparable. As we grew older, everyone assumed he and I would marry and have a family of our own. But what happened to my daddy changed everything. Momma was scared for me, wanted me to go away. She said I'd have a better life up North with family there. I didn't want to go, didn't want to leave her, and I didn't want to leave Henry."

"But you sat here and gave me advice about living up North. You listened to my fears and excitement. And you never told me. And Henry did the same thing. He knew how much I admired you, and *he* never said anything."

"Nell, you don't understand. Our parents wanted us to marry, and most folks around these parts expected us to. But Henry and I didn't feel that way about each other. I loved him like a big brother, still do. It's like how you love Robert. Once he attempted to act the way others wanted us to—to be romantic and such. I remember we were sitting at the river on a warm spring day. We'd been wading in the water, picking up stones to add to the collection I kept on our front porch. My daddy hated the mess I made with those rocks. I left them spread out, so I could pick them up to examine and rearrange according to size and color. Sometimes Daddy'd accidentally step on the stones and lose his balance. He'd grumble under his breath. Momma would rush to scoop them out of his way, then scold me and threaten to toss the rocks back into the river.

"That day, as we sat on a large rock, kicking water, Henry began to rub my leg. He didn't look at me, nor I at him. He just kept touching me in a peculiar way. His fingers had a wanting to them in the pressure and motion as he rubbed up and down. I didn't know what to do. Then he tried to kiss me. Our lips just briefly brushed before I jumped up and ran away. I left my shoes and socks at the water and ran all the way home, bounded into my room, threw myself on the bed, and wept."

"What'd you tell your mother?"

"Never told her what happened. About a week later he came by the house with my shoes and socks. When I came out of the house, we both struggled to find words. I took my things from him and turned to go back inside. I heard him say, 'I'm sorry.' Eventually we became brother and sister again, although it took a while. We never spoke about that day, or the failed kiss. Our parents came to realize we weren't meant to be wed and accepted our sibling-like relationship for what it was."

"It sounds as though he did have feelings for you, beyond brotherly ones."

"That may be so, but you're the one he married, not me."

"I don't understand him, Miss Parker. We've been married almost two years, we have two babies, and I can't figure out who he is."

"I could tell from your letters something wasn't right.

You never mentioned Henry. It was as if you were alone until the children came along, and then it's just been the two of them and you. Sometimes it made me sad to read your letters. When a woman writes as deftly as you do and omits mention of her husband, it's a profound statement."

"Can you help me?"

"Oh, Nell, you're asking an unmarried woman with no children to help you figure out marriage and motherhood. I don't think I'm the best one for this."

"But you can help me understand Henry. I need that most of all."

"Is he silent with you?"

"Yes."

"Is he hurtful toward you?"

"Only in the silence and not wanting me to leave the apartment."

"What do you mean?"

"He doesn't want me to know other people or go outside. He won't even get a telephone. At least I have a little transistor radio so I can listen to music and the news. The few friends I have aren't allowed to visit except one day a week. And he leaves me every Sunday for church and won't even share what the sermon was."

"You and the children don't go to church?"

"No."

"But church is a big part of a family's life."

"I know . . . but he said I shouldn't go, so I don't."

"You do whatever Henry says?"

"Yes. Aren't I supposed to?"

"The question is—is that how you want to live?"

"No, it isn't. But I don't know how to change things. I

tried once, had that reading job at the library, did some work at Ginny's beauty shop. But he snatched it all away from me."

"Nell, I think Henry is a kind and tortured soul at the same time. He's never had much, and going North held so much promise for him—at least in his mind. I don't think he's achieved the life he thought he'd find there—filled with great success, a large family, and a close circle of friends."

"We certainly don't have any of that."

"My best advice—you have to be the woman you're meant to be. You can't allow yourself to disappear in his shadow. That's not who you are, not who your daddy wanted you to be. Find yourself, Nell. I know you can."

SUNDAY MORNING SNUCK up on me like an old friend I hadn't visited with in a long time but was uncertain about seeing. I was lying in bed, listening to Momma hum the hymns that she and the other church women would raise their voices to sing during the service today, leading everyone in heavenly hallelujahs, yes Jesus, praise the Lord, and amens. I could hear my brothers and sisters as they got dressed in their Sunday best and prepared the little ones for the day of worship and fellowship. My heart was racing, but my limbs were numb. I pulled the covers over my head, pressed my eyes shut, and tried to silence the deafening noise of family greeting a Sunday with such certain joy and familiarity.

"Baby Girl," Momma said as she poked her head into my room, "why aren't you up and dressed? We's got to get to church. I need to be there early with the choir."

"Not going," I mumbled from under the covers.

"Of course you're going, now get up."

I didn't move, just curled myself into a knot and rolled against the wall, hoping she'd leave me alone. But she sat on the bed and started to rub my back, just the way I remembered she'd do whenever I was hurt or sad or scared. She kept right on humming and then patted my head with the palm of her hand. It was that gesture, so comforting and gentle, so full of the warmth I'd missed for the past two years, so full of both her and Daddy's essence, caring for their Baby Girl with unconditional love, that brought the torrent of tears. I heaved and gasped for air in my chest, wiggled over to her, pulled my head out from the covers, and buried my face in her lap.

"Baby Girl, calm down," she said as she handed me her hankie to wipe my face and blow my nose. "Why don't you want to go to church?"

"It's not church, Momma. I don't want to go home!" I howled and sank my head into her lap again.

"We talked about this. You're a wife and momma now; you belong with the family that you done made. Now I need to leave—we'll bring your little ones with us. Pull yourself together; people want to see you."

She got up to leave before I was finished crying; it felt as though she was disgusted with me for being pitiful. But then she bent over, hugged me, and said, "I've never known scared to be in the same place as you, Baby Girl. I want to make you feel better, but there's not much I can do. And this isn't where you belong anymore. Everything Daddy and I taught you is right here and here." She tapped my head and heart. "It's up to you to not give it all away like some orphan who's been robbed of her last worldly possession."

## Chapter Fifteen

CHURCH HAD BEEN ON MY MIND EVERY DAY SINCE I returned from seeing Momma. The way she'd looked at me, never saying anything in reprimand but knowing all along that I was not doing the things she expected of me. The truth of that was weighing heavily on me. It was as awkward as moving around with the new baby that was forming in my belly, my ankles swollen, my stomach uneasy again all day. Momma hadn't made a fuss with me, she had just told me to be true to how she and Daddy had raised me, to remember that we should be thankful for all God does for us. She told me that I needed the right tools to bring this message to the children, her grandbabies.

"I want to go to church," I said to Henry on Saturday night, as I watched him polish his Sunday shoes. The words were out of my mouth before I could catch them, ball them up in my fist, and shove them in the pocket of my cotton dress.

When he heard my words, he stopped and glared at me. "What'd you say?"

"It's time I started to attend church, to meet other women, to pray to the Lord in his house. It's time, Henry."

"What about the babies?"

"They're welcome in the Lord's house too."

"How old are you?"

"What?"

"I said, how old are you to be making statements like this to me? You're just a child yourself. You've been acting different since you been back home."

"I'm old enough to be your wife and these children's momma, old enough to be carrying another child inside of me. Old enough to cook and clean all day. Momma wanted to know what our church was like. There was nothing I could say. It made me ashamed. Church is an important part of a family's life. I won't let you deny me that any longer. I'm going to church!"

My voice echoed round the apartment, ricocheting from wall to wall, claiming its territory. Henry's nose flared for just a moment, reacting to the unexpected strength of my words as though they were too pungent, making his eyes water. I held my breath, not certain if he'd lash out at me, but I steeled my back, ready to fight if necessary.

He studied my face as though he were trying to hear the conversation between Momma and me and said, "What'd you tell Momma and the others about me?"

"The truth," I said with my chin thrust in the air. "I spoke with everyone about our life, even Miss Parker."

In the early days of our courtship I had often felt as though I had Henry's full attention, as though I were the only person his eyes could focus on, mine the only voice his ears wanted to hear. I'd lost that sense somewhere between the bus trip north and the ensuing isolation that had become my life. Yet at this moment I felt fierce attention coming from him as he contemplated what I'd said to my family.

"What'd you tell them?" He stepped to within an inch of me. Hot air coming from his nostrils stung my cheeks as he clenched and unclenched his fists. "What!" Spittle hit my face as he shouted.

I began to back away, gaining more distance between our bodies so the force of his anger had someplace to go. But something inside made me stand firm. Maybe it was the recollection of Momma's words, or Miss Parker's advice about being the woman I was meant to be, or the new life squirming inside of me while the other two children played on the floor, reminding me that my life was about to get smaller yet again. For an instant I heard Daddy's voice telling me that he loved me, that I always made him proud. I took a step toward Henry, with my hands on my hips, and said, "I gave up my home and family to come here with you and be your wife. I'm having your babies, cleaning this tiny place we call a home, cooking your meals, taking care of your manly needs. And all the while you treat me like a prisoner or, worse, your personal slave. The slaves were freed a long time ago! I won't be treated this way any longer. I deserve better, and I intend to have better. That's what I told the family."

"How dare you speak poorly of me. Easy for you to do that without me there to keep you in your place. Woman, you're lucky to have a man at all, never mind one as good as me. You got food on the table, a place to lay your head, regular loving, and a family to care for. What more do you need? Do you know how many woman out there want what I have to give?"

"I don't know *out there* at all, since you snatched the outside world away from me, keep me locked away like some bird you torture by clipping its wings. How would I know if anyone wants you or not? All I know is that things need to change around here, or else!"

"Or else what? You threatening me?"

"I'm telling you! I can't live this way any longer."

"You're the one who went around lying, doing things at Ginny's and the library, disobeying me. I've never done a thing like that. I go to work, come home, take care of you and the babies. I do what a man supposed to do for his family. You stepped out. How do I know you weren't looking at another man?"

"You know I wasn't! Don't try to turn this around. We need to make this marriage work for both of us, not just for you." Exhaustion was beginning to seep into my veins. I wanted to keep up the argument and force Henry to change at that very moment, but I knew the only thing I could possibly change was myself.

The children were both crying as the harsh words we spewed at one another disturbed their playing. They wailed above our shouts, so loudly I thought the neighbors might start banging on the floor to get us to quiet down or else call the police, thinking a murder was taking place in this apartment that was normally so quiet.

Henry looked at the children as though he were about to say something to them, then looked at me. His shoulders sagged as he rubbed his eyes. He sat down on the foot of the bed and picked up the shoe-polishing materials again. I could see him start to disappear into the leather, dirty cloth, polish, and newspaper laid on the floor to hold his work. Or perhaps it was the children and I who were doing the disappearing. In a voice so quiet I could barely hear him, he said, "What do you want? I don't know how else to be."

"I want to go to church. I want the children to be christened. I want Sunday to be our family church day. That'd be a start."

THE CHURCH WAS ten blocks from our house, a quick walk if you're a man strolling alone. However, with a pregnant wife and two children in tow, it became an ordeal for Henry. He shouted over his shoulder, "Hurry up. You're going to make me miss the opening hymn."

Junior, April, and I trailed behind Henry. I alternated between carrying April in my arms and on my back, while yanking Junior's hand as we raced to keep up. I thought, *I need a baby stroller.* The few times Henry and I had taken the children out he had always carried them, leaving me free to wander beside him and enjoy being outdoors. Today my feet felt like two small tree stumps thudding against unforgiving cement. The children became low-hanging fruit ready to drop to the ground at any moment. My face stung from the wind of Henry's energy pushing past his back to my nose. My hair was matted to my forehead in streams of sweat.

"Henry, slow down," I panted. "We can't keep up with you. Slow down."

"Keep up, woman. You wanted to come to church—well, this is it."

As best I could determine the church was divine, but as I looked around through the film of dust that had collected on my eyes and the stinging sweat that I tried to sop up with my dress, everything seemed blurred. When we'd left the apartment, I'd thought the three of us looked to be in good shape, but compared to the women, children, and men in their Sunday best, we looked as if we should've had tin cups in our hands.

Henry greeted the minister who stood at the top of the steps. He said hello to the other church-goers, then disappeared inside. He never looked back for me or the children. He was the butler making a targeted entrance, and I was the weary field-hand hoping for a chance to enter the big house and see the master.

"Hello—Miss . . . ?" The Reverend extended his hand to me. He was wearing a dark blue suit, a starched white shirt, and a blue tie with a small, gold, diamond-shaped pattern running down the center. He had a full round belly bursting against the buttons of his suit jacket, straining the threads. His face was round and dark as a blackberry; his warm smile reached from one deep-set dimple to the other.

"Mrs. Bight," I said. "This is Junior and April, our young ones."

"You would be Henry's family, wife and children, then?"

"Yes, we are."

"My, my. Mrs. Leonard, come here and meet Mr. Bight's family."

"Henry's family?" A tall, slender, elegant woman walked up to the Reverend. She put her arm through his and looked at me. She had on the most beautiful Sunday hat I'd ever seen. It looked to be silk, with crinoline billowing around the sides and trailing down the back of her neck. Her dress matched the light green color of the ribbon on the hat, and her white gloves extended to her elbows. A small purse at her wrist and high-heeled shoes completed her Sunday attire. "Hello, dear. Such a pleasure to meet you. Welcome to our church. The Reverend and I are so happy to finally meet Mr. Bight's family."

"I'm glad to be here. Henry tells me about your husband's sermons."

"Mrs. Leonard, perhaps you could show Mrs. Bight to the ladies' room. She may want to, well, tidy up a bit before taking her seat with her husband," the Reverend said.

"Of course," Mrs. Leonard responded.

Only then did I feel the shabbiness of my Sunday attire—old dusty shoes with a broken buckle, a cotton house dress that had seen too many washings and was now sporting a wet, dark area down the front, my hatless head with wind-blown hair sticking up in all directions. As I watched her examine the babies and me, the corners of my eyes started to sting. "I'm sorry," I whispered to my feet. "We don't belong here, not like this. Maybe next Sunday."

Mrs. Leonard touched my shoulder. "You belong here, Mrs. Bight. And your children as well. This is the Lord's house—all are welcome." She hugged my shaking frame and led us downstairs.

We passed through a large open area with tables and chairs arranged in banquet style. "We have lunches and dinners here," Mrs. Leonard told me, "and in here is the playroom for children too young to sit through the church service." She pointed to a room off to the right, which had toys, books, and small tables. There were several children in cribs, and a young woman was sitting with them, reading from bible storybooks. "Junior and April can stay here, if you like. Or you can keep them with you and Mr. Bight during service."

"I think they'll stay with us."

"That's fine, dear. Now here is a closet with some dresses; there's probably something in your size. And on the shelf are children's clothes. If you look in the boxes on the floor, you'll find all manner of shoes. Surely a pair or two will fit you and the children."

I didn't move to the closet.

When she looked over her shoulder and saw the look on my face, she said, "It's all right, dear. We all have needs sometimes, and the Lord provides. The church is a place where we take care of one another. Why, I'm sure in no time at all you and Mr. Bight will be adding to this collection for someone else in the church to benefit from."

I inched closer to the closet, keeping my eyes fixed on hers. "Well, there may be something—for the children, of course."

"Take your time. I'll be in the kitchen, right through those doors to the left. When you're ready, just get me and I'll show you our powder room."

The closet was stuffed with pretty dresses, men's suits, jackets, coats, children's clothes, shoes in all colors and sizes lined up neatly on the floor, and hats on the top shelf. There were more clothes in this closet than I'd ever seen, even in our house back on the farm, where a dozen people lived on and off. I settled Junior and April on the floor and touched one of the dresses. The material was soft. It slid through my fingers like water flowing from a well pump. Then I began to run my hand over the fabric of all the dresses. It was like being in the library, feeling the bindings of books against my fingertips, except the cloth was delicate, inviting in a new way. I began to imagine myself dancing, twirling in one dress after another while others admired me.

I picked out clothes for the children, with shoes to

match. Then I found just the right dress for me. It was sky-blue, with a ribbon around the waist and a row of buttons down the back. It was the finest one in the closet, the very first one I had touched. I didn't know if the things would fit, but after Mrs. Leonard got us settled in the ladies' room, we tried everything on. It took my breath away to see how we looked—like a real family dressed properly for church. We managed to look almost as good as we had when we went to church with Momma and the family. Even then, I'd had to borrow clothes for me and the children. But those clothes were farm fabrics, worn thin in the seams, still carrying the scents of hard work and dirt. These items had the smell of Northern progress, the promise of more.

"Now let me help you with your hair—if you don't mind, that is," Mrs. Leonard offered.

I immediately thought about Ginny. She and the girls had stopped coming by the apartment to visit. It was gradual, the way one minute you have a full glass of water and then slowly the water empties from sipping and natural evaporation. With each visit there was less and less to say. I only had the daily goings-on with the children to discuss, while the girls' lives were as full as ever with stories about their customers and the neighborhood. I think at some point they just decided we had lost anything in common and that sitting in my tiny apartment had become stifling. So the glass emptied, like the other glasses in my life—the library, my family, even Daddy. All that was left was a collection of empty drinking vessels resting on a shelf, smudged with lip and fingerprint memories.

Mrs. Leonard's fingers were gentle in my hair. She didn't have the professional lilt to her movements as Ginny had, but it was comforting to let someone else manage my hair again.

"When is your baby due?"

"In a few months."

"Three children—my, my. You and Mr. Bight certainly have a full house."

"Henry wants a large family. At least seven children."

"Seven!"

"Henry says a man and a woman should bring lots of young ones into the world. Back home you needed to have as many children as possible to work the farm. But here in the city, I don't know why so many children are needed. But Henry says we should keep making babies."

"What do you say?"

"Nothing so far. I'm still thinking on it."

"I see. Will you be coming to church every Sunday?"

"I hope to. This is my first time, but you know that. Henry wanted me to be safe, to wait for him at home."

"I see."

"I take care of the family, everything in the house. Henry takes care of all the outside things that need taking care of. He enjoys coming to church."

"I see. And what do you enjoy doing?"

"I cook real good, clean, keep the babies happy."

"What stores do you like to shop at?"

"Henry does all the shopping."

"I see. Nell—may I call you Nell? And please, call me Phyllis."

"Yes."

"Nell, why don't you join our women's group at church? We meet once a week to plan activities each month, but mostly we're close friends who look out for one another. We have lunches, go shopping together, visit one another in our homes. It would be good to have someone new, and so young, become part of our group."

"I don't know. I have to take care of my babies. And I'm not sure how Henry would feel about me going out."

"Hmm . . . maybe in time, then. A mother, yes, and so young! Little Mother Nell, that's who you are. Tell me, what do you think of your hairstyle?"

Phyllis turned me around to face the mirror. My raggedy braids were gone. Since visiting Momma I had reverted back to the basic braid hairstyle that was easiest for me to manage. Phyllis had made a French twist with my hair, using lots of bobby-pins and hairspray to hold it in place. All the hair was pulled off my face, so my high forehead was emphasized. I looked older, sophisticated, like someone who belonged in the fine dress I was wearing.

"Phyllis, thank you. I look like someone else."

"You're quite attractive; you just need to let your features shine through."

"My school-teacher back home looked pretty. I always admired her, how she dressed and carried herself. I saw her recently when I went back home to visit after my daddy passed away."

"My condolences on losing your father."

"Thank you."

"Did you finish school?"

"My family married me off to Henry. We left the South and came up here."

"Are you attending school now?"

"No, I don't have time, and I don't need schooling."

"Henry told you this?"

"Yes. But I like to read."

"Is that so? What kind of books do you read?"

"All kinds. Love stories, mysteries—anything I can find. I read those stories to the babies all the time. They know the characters as well as I do."

"We have a room full of books right here in the church. You can look through those and read whatever you like. There's also a library nearby."

"Henry took me to the library when we first moved here. I got my very own library card. It was such a beautiful place, full of so many books. I even spent time reading to a group of children once a week. I enjoyed that; it reminded me of how I felt in the classroom back home. But I haven't been back there since . . ."

"I take it Henry doesn't want you to go there alone?'

"That's right. He worries about the babies and me, but he brings books home for me when I want new ones. Do you and Reverend Leonard have children?"

"No, I'm afraid not. By the time we married it was too late for babies. All the children of our church-members are our children. Now Junior and April will become a part of the family too."

She picked up April, and Junior and I headed upstairs to greet the congregation—and to find Henry.

When we approached the pew where Henry was seated, he casually looked up from the prayer book. Then he dropped his program, turned sideways in the pew, and rose to greet Mrs. Leonard and us, his family. She waved her hand for him to stay seated, then said to me, "Take your place with your husband, dear."

I slid into the pew to sit beside Henry with April and

Junior next to me. Henry stared at me, taking into account the fine dress I was wearing, my new hairdo, the good clothes his children had on.

Mrs. Leonard sauntered to the very first pew and took her place directly in front of her husband. As soon as she was settled, Reverend Leonard stood to begin the church service.

I was transported to the last Sunday service I had attended with Momma and the family in our small, hot church in the center of town. I remembered then how as children we would get to Sunday School early in the morning, have our bible studies, then join the adults as the main service began, several hours later. My momma and all the women of the church wore their Sunday best and always carried fans provided by the local funeral parlor, to move the humid air away from their cheeks as the minister preached. The choir sang gospels, and we clapped and sang along. Sweat poured from everyone's brow. We prayed aloud with the minister, shouted hallelujah as the sermon delivered important messages, acknowledged those church-members who were ill or in hard times, broke bread and drank wine to honor the life of Christ, stood up in praise, kneeled in prayer, cried for forgiveness, hugged one another in greeting—and we did this each and every Sunday.

When I had joined Momma and the family at church just a week ago, I'd realized how much I was missing. Now I was in our church in the North with my family, the first important step in a new approach to my life. I wiped tears from my eyes and blew my nose. Henry's back stiffened. It was then that I heard Reverend Leonard formally welcome us. He said, "I'm so pleased to greet Mrs. Bight and the lovely Bight children in our church. We all know Mr. Bight is a long-standing member of this congregation, giving his time and love to all. I expect, as we come to know Mrs. Bight and their children, they too will be treasured family members. Let us pray." The Reverend's prayer of welcome filled the room and he finished with, "Let the church say amen."

When the choir finished the final song, everyone turned in their pews to say hello to those sitting beside, in front, and behind them, saying, "God be with you." Henry turned to greet the family sitting behind us, but he didn't introduce me or the children, so I introduced myself. I did the same with the people sitting in front of us. I started to look to Henry for an indication that it was time to leave, but he was looking away from me, so I guided the children to the center aisle and followed people to the front door, where the Reverend and Mrs. Leonard were chatting with parishioners as they said their good-byes. Henry was behind us.

When we reached the door, Mrs. Leonard gave me a gentle hug and asked, "Did you enjoy the service?"

"Oh, yes, it was wonderful. It made me think about my family and our church in Louisiana."

"We'll see you next Sunday, of course?" As she spoke these words, Henry approached her side. "Mr. Bight," she added, "I've enjoyed meeting your wife. She's lovely. And your children are the cutest ever. We look forward to seeing them every Sunday. I plan on stopping by this week. In fact, I'll bring some of the members from our ladies' group. We can welcome Mrs. Bight to the congregation and see if there is any way we can assist her with connecting to others in the neighborhood. Will that be all right with you, dear?" She never took her eyes off Henry as she posed this question to me.

"Of course—thank you," I said.

"And we can take you to all the shops we frequent for clothes and things for the home. Would you like to go shopping with us?" Her eyes were fixed on Henry as she asked this.

"Yes, I'd like that." I turned to Henry and said, "Henry?"

"I guess that's a good idea," he said, looking at Mrs. Leonard.

"Well, it's settled. Mrs. Bight, the ladies and I will see you on Thursday." With that she placed my arm through Henry's and shooed us out the door and down the steps.

Reverend Leonard shook Henry's hand and said, "So glad to meet your family, Mr. Bight. You must be proud of your wife and children. We'll see all of you next Sunday."

We walked down the steps arm in arm. Henry was carrying April. Junior was holding my hand. It was a perfect picture of a perfect young family walking home from a perfect Sunday service on a perfect sunny day.

Suddenly Henry shifted April from his right arm to his left, letting my arm drop to my side. In a low voice, muffled because he was talking to me through April's body, he said, "Where'd you get those clothes?"

"From Mrs. Leonard, the closet downstairs in the church. There were many nice things there. The church members look out for one another by bringing clothes, shoes, and hats for those who may need them."

"My family doesn't wear other people's clothes. We don't wear hand-me-downs. It's shameful."

"But I don't have good clothes. I—we need good clothes for church."

"Who says you're going to church again?"

"I do. Mrs. Leonard and Reverend Leonard expect to see us again. I will be coming to church, Henry."

We walked in silence for the next block. Henry was bouncing April in his arms as if he were giving her a ride on a merry-go-ground. He said, "I'll buy some clothes this week, your own dresses and things."

I took a deep breath, knowing what I needed to say and unsure if I could force the words out of my mouth. "I want to buy my own clothes."

Henry stopped, turned to face me. "What?" he said.

"I want to buy my own clothes."

"With what? You don't have any money of your own. You don't know anything about clothing stores. What're you talking about, woman?"

I looked up the street to my right and then to my left, thinking that a solution might be out there and that I could just pluck it like a spring blossom, lose myself in the bouquet of its scent, show it to Henry. But the sidewalks were barren of flowers. Looking down at my feet, I said, "I could get a job, earn my own money. I know how to do things. Then I can buy my own clothes and things for the children too. Ginny would take me back, working for her."

"No wife of mine is working."

I couldn't find a response in the tips of my shoes, or the cracks in the sidewalk, or the weeds peeking out from small lines of dirt. No answer lived in the palms of my hands or the tears dripping down my cheeks, making small marks on my new dress as they fell from my face. Yet suddenly, with a heavy tug in my stomach, I discovered the words from thinking about the characters in my books, and from reflecting on Mrs. Leonard and her charms and grace. I found the words

in the encouragement that both Momma and Miss Parker
had given me about finding myself.

"Henry, if you don't want me to wear other people's
clothes, then you have to give me money of my own, because
I'm going to church every Sunday."

Henry looked up and down the street, searching for so-
lutions the way I'd done a moment ago. The sidewalk was
barren for him as well. Days seemed to pass in the heavy
silence hanging between us as we stood facing one another.
Junior and April were tired and hungry, but they kept still,
waiting for some motion from their parents.

"You sassing me?" Henry said.

"No such thing as a grown woman, wife, and mother
sassing her husband," I replied.

Henry grunted. We walked home in silence.

Once the children were asleep that night, Henry and I
lay down together. He started to pull at me as was his way,
not saying a word, not kissing, just wanting to force me on
my back, spread my legs, and shove himself inside.

I stopped him and said, "I'd like us to make love."

He rolled onto his back, his arm across his face, and said,
"What'd you think we've been doing all this time?" His lips
didn't move; he spoke through his teeth.

"Having sex, that's all. I want loving, Henry."

"Jesus, woman!"

"Don't use the Lord's name in vain! You know we don't
make love—you just take me, you don't give anything tender
in return. I want that."

"Since when?"

"Since I decided it's time for me to be a grown woman."

"How am I supposed to know these things? One day

everything is fine, the next day I can't do anything right."

"From now on, I'll let you know what I need."

"Great." He turned his back to me.

We didn't have sex or make love that night. I had the most peaceful sleep I'd had since marrying Henry. Our marriage license, filed in a city-hall office in Louisiana, was dated two and a half years earlier. It stated that two consenting adults had entered into the legal marriage union. But in actuality only one adult had been present that day. Rightfully, this day's date should have been the one recorded.

# Chapter Sixteen

IT WAS WRONG. I KNEW IT THEN. I KNOW IT NOW. It was wrong. Criminal as swarming locusts ravaging crop fields in the height of growing season. That happened one summer in Louisiana. We'd heard stories about how they came from nowhere, cast a thick humming cloud around the sun, spread a mammoth shadow over entire fields and towns, swooped down on crops, ate and ate until they tired of the fruits nurtured by the back-breaking work of farm owners and field hands, then disappeared mysteriously, leaving farmers with poverty the coming winter.

When they arrived that summer, we were sitting on the porch, the men talking and joking, my momma and sisters resting after preparing and cleaning up after dinner, me on the steps with a book to read. At first it sounded like a harmonica, played by someone with an inexhaustible amount of air in his lungs. The same monstrous note grew louder, danced through the air, piercing our eardrums. When we stepped off the porch and looked in the sky in the direction of the noise, we gasped at the fast-moving dark mass of thousands of insects headed our way. "Locusts! Locusts! Get into the house!" Daddy hollered. "Close up the doors and windows. Put cloth in all the cracks!" We scattered, obeying his orders without a second thought.

We stood in a tight circle in the middle of the kitchen, holding onto one another as though the house were about to be yanked from its foundation and hurtled into the air, leaving us exposed. Suddenly the locusts hit. It sounded like bullets from machine guns pelting the walls and roof. The insects forced their way into the house. My daddy and brothers swatted and crushed them with their work shoes, and I screamed in terror. My momma held me tight and said, "Hush up. It'll be over soon. They can't hurt us."

And it was over rapidly, almost as soon as it had begun. We peeked outside and watched the tail end of the swarm make its way further north, away from our farm. My daddy stood with his back to the us, surveyed the damage to his crops, wiped his brow, and said, "It's criminal, all of our work eaten by these insects. We're gonna have a hard winter." There was nothing left for us to eat or store for the winter months, nothing for us to sell at market. My momma was mistaken. The bugs did harm us. Every time we opened a cabinet and a stray bug fell down, every time the wind blew a few dead insects from the gutter to the porch steps, every time we heard the crunch of a decaying carcass under our feet as we walked in the fields, we knew it was wrong, we didn't deserve this.

I SHOULD HAVE pulled away from him the first time he rubbed up against me. We were in the church kitchen, preparing food for the communion dinner to take place after church services. The church ladies were comfortable letting me become the "lady of the kitchen." It was such a joy for me to be part of the church in this way, one of the favored ladies with many friends. I was happy to have friends. *Mother Nell*—that was what everyone affectionately called me. Phyllis's nickname had stuck, partly because of who she was and the influence she had with everyone, but also because I kept getting pregnant.

I lost one baby in the first trimester. My body didn't want to keep that little one; the tiny motionless mass flushed out of me one night. The doctor assured us there was nothing wrong with me, I would be able to carry a baby to term again. With only one son and a daughter, Henry needed assurances that I could deliver him more sons. "Maybe your body needs a rest," he said after our visit to the doctor. "We'll take some time before having another baby."

"Time" turned out to be twelve months. It was the first year during our marriage that I didn't carry another person in my belly. It was the year of my twentieth birthday. Then Teddy arrived.

Henry wanted more sons, as though he were running a large farm and needed a house full of strong field hands. Nature had a different idea. I had three miscarriages after Teddy was born. The doctor told us my body was too exhausted and worn out to carry any more babies to full term. He said it was dangerous for me to get pregnant again. Once Henry heard this, he stopped touching me, looking at me, having sex with me. Our bed became dry and parched, but my thirst continued.

I should have pulled away from him, but instead I leaned into him as his arm brushed against the soft tender flesh of my arm, a tender spot just above my freshly shaved armpit, skin that didn't often get exposed to outside elements, skin sensitive to the delicate brush of fabric, with tingling nerve endings. I was reaching for a box on the top shelf of a cabinet. He was standing beside me, watching. Watching me was how he spent his time Sunday afternoons, as I worked in the kitchen.

Charles was the oldest son of one of the congregation's families. When he graduated from high school, he went to college—the first young person from the neighborhood to do so. He earned a degree in psychology and had hopes of staying on to obtain a master's degree, but when his daddy took ill, he returned home. He'd grown up in the church, so when he came back to the neighborhood, he immediately took his place there.

Phyllis introduced us. "Charles, this is Mrs. Bight, a new member since you were here. She and her husband moved into the neighborhood last year."

He took my hand in his, tipped his hat, and said, "Hello, Mrs. Bight. I'm pleased to meet you."

We stared at each other for too long. "Mrs. Bight has several children," Phyllis said, interrupting our electric pause, "all growing up as part of our church family. Her husband, Mr. Bight, has been a well-respected member of the congregation for some time. I'll take you to meet him." And with that she whisked Charles away.

But soon he volunteered to help in the kitchen—there were crates of cans that needed moving, boxes to be carried, heavy pots to lift, trash to be taken outside . . . and me to brush up against.

My knees became weak when I felt his flesh glide against my inner arm. I shifted my weight against the cabinet, lost my balance, and began to fall. He caught me by the waist, holding me against his chest. "You all right?" he asked.

I could feel his belt buckle pressing against me through my cotton dress.

"Yes. I suddenly felt dizzy."

"Maybe you need to sit down." But he didn't let go of my waist, didn't move me away from him to a chair. He continued to press against my upper body. I melted into him. Beads of sweat formed on the tip of my nose; my cheeks began to burn. I closed my eyes as I felt his warm breath on my forehead.

"Nell, are you all right?" Phyllis came running over. She gently led me to a nearby chair. "Sit down—I'll get you some water. Charles, see if Doctor Kendal is still in the church."

"I don't need a doctor, just lost my balance. I'll be fine."

"Charles, maybe you should go now. Leave me to look after Nell."

"Yes, Mrs. Leonard."

I stared at the floor as he walked away, anxiously listening to his footsteps as the sound became fainter and fainter.

"Nell, you're a married woman with a house full of children. What're you thinking?" Mrs. Leonard whispered in my face, while holding onto my shoulders.

"What do you mean?"

"You know perfectly well what I mean. This is the Lord's house. You are a Godly woman, a married woman."

"It's just that . . . Henry and I . . . we don't. . . . It's been over a year since he's touched me. He's afraid I'll get pregnant again. So he refuses to touch me, and he won't use any birth control. And Charles is so young, so—"

"Nell! It's wrong. Go home to your family. Do not shame yourself or this church. Understand?"

"Yes."

"Do you?"

"Yes. Phyllis, please don't be angry with me."

"Just go home, Nell, to your husband and children."

THE NEXT SUNDAY I asked Phyllis if it would be okay if I came back on Wednesday nights to work in the kitchen and the children's space—just to keep up with things. Last Sunday, Charles had grabbed my arm as I headed to the ladies' room before going home and pulled me into a corner under the stairs. He whispered, "Nell, I want to see you." He suggested that we could spend time together, one night a week, to get to know each other. We could talk about books and our lives. I hesitated at first, but the thought of being with a man who was educated, who was interested in my thoughts, who made the hair dance on my legs and arms and the back of my neck—I wanted to have this.

"Seems to me we get everything done on Sunday afternoons," Phyllis said.

"You know there's always something that needs doing. I'm happy to give more time—just one night a week," I replied.

Phyllis put away the pot she'd been drying, rubbed her hands on the apron, and walked over to where I was standing by the stove. With a quizzical look on her face she asked, "Charles have anything to do with this?"

"Charles! No, this is about me wanting to be as helpful as I can. And honestly, I'd welcome the peace and quiet."

"Nell, I don't know what you're cooking up, but be careful."

"I'll be fine, Phyllis."

I bumped into Charles in the vestibule and slipped a note into his hand: "Wednesday nights at 6," it read.

Wednesday night arrived, and I raced back to the church. I asked Henry to watch the children, saying, "Phyllis needs me to finish some chores." I expected him to tell me that it was my job to care for the little ones, that I should stay home; but he just acquiesced, said he was tired, he'd put the children down and go to bed early.

Charles was waiting for me, but he didn't hear me walk into the room. I watched him for a moment, enjoying the look of his face as he read from a book propped up on the table. He was holding the book and sitting just as a student would in a classroom, hoping for the teacher to admire his posture and attention to studies. His eyes seemed to dance from word to word, line to line, as though he were eagerly absorbing each image created by stringing the words together.

"I almost thought you weren't coming tonight," he said without looking up.

"I didn't think you knew I was here."

"I was aware of you from the moment you stepped inside the building. Come here, sit by me." He pulled a chair out, rising as I walked toward him.

"What're you reading?" I asked.

"*All God's Children Got Traveling Feet*, by Maya Angelou."

"I don't know that one. I read her first book, *I Know Why the Caged Bird Sings*. It was beautiful and sad."

"But joyful and triumphant. All of her work has a positive lilt to it, even when the circumstances are less than favorable."

"I think that's why I enjoyed her book. It reminded me of life as I know it."

"Any trouble leaving the house?"

"No, it was easier than I thought it'd be. Henry agreed to watch the children."

"Is he a good man, your husband?"

"I'd rather not talk about the family."

"What do you want to discuss?"

"You. Tell me about your life. I want to hear about college—what's that like?"

"It's a lot like church, actually. A group of people come together on a regular basis, share stories and experiences, get preached to, and then go away in the hopes of applying what they've learned. Then they come back together and compare notes. Probably more gossip happens on campus than at church, but that may not be true. The biggest difference between a college campus and the church is that there are more young people at college. Here it seems like everyone's old, like decrepit grandparents."

"Don't you like it here?"

"I miss being around my friends, miss college life. My plan was to stay on and get a master's degree, but I was pulled back here when my father died. I'm glad to help out my mother, but it's just not what I expected I'd be doing right now."

"I lost my daddy too. I think about him all the time. Momma has family around her, so I didn't need to move back. But I did spend time with her, and it was sad to see how she's changed since Daddy passed. Death changes things."

"That it does, but let's not talk about sad things. I understand you like to read."

"I read all the time, and I have some favorite books—

classics, I think they're called. My schoolteacher introduced me to the love of reading. I hope to see my children become readers too."

"No talk about the family, remember? I brought a book for you that I think you'll like. If you can read it by next week, we can talk about it Wednesday. Think you can do that?"

"Yes. What's it about?"

"*Lady Chatterley's Lover*, by D. H. Lawrence. A true classic, about a man and a woman who meet and fall in love." He handed me the book and helped me up. "We should get going." He stood so close I could take in the scent of him. He placed a gentle kiss on my cheek, then turned and left.

I clutched the book to my chest and continued to savor his scent lingering in the air, and then touched the spot where his lips had brushed my skin.

RAIN PELTED AGAINST the house in endless streams that created rivulets on the sidewalk and puddles of mud in the back yard. The tomatoes in the garden strained against their stems, as if trying to keep their green skins away from the ground long enough for the rains to cease, so they could escape rotting. I welcomed the chill and damp that engulfed the neighborhood as I sat by the back door, poring over Charles's gift. Reading the story, which was pregnant with the aroma of thick moist forests, leaves dancing on seldom-trodden trails, sensual trysts in a vine-covered shelter, caused my body to stir.

I had wanted to begin reading the night I returned from meeting Charles, but fear, or perhaps the expectation of excitement, kept me from touching the book while Henry was in the house. The brief description of the two lovers on the dust cover and the image of a man and woman entwined like weeds in an untamed forest were like promises that the story would carry me to places I'd want to languish in alone. And so I sat at the backdoor, Henry's shoe-cleaning items to my left, the sink full of pots and pans at my back, the little garden in view but barely visible through the sheets of rain, the children fast asleep for their first nap of the day—and devoured every word of my prized gift.

We were in an actual house now, not the tiny apartment that had defined my world for years. With three children, their toys, cribs, clothes, and two adults, we just couldn't live any longer in a place meant for just one person.

One day Henry had come home and announced, "We're moving. You need to get everything packed so we can be out of here before the next rent payment is due."

"Where're we going?" I asked.

"Home, our own house. We need more room. It's getting so I can't find an empty spot in this apartment to sit down. The children are growing fast, and there'll be more to come. We need a house for our family."

"How can we afford a house?"

"Not *buying*, just moving—we'll be renting, like here. A guy at work, his mother passed away months back, and her house has been sitting empty; he doesn't need it but doesn't want to sell yet. I asked if he'd consider renting, and he said yes. Won't cost much more than this place—he's giving me a good deal. I just need to take care of it and save him some money, in exchange for reasonable rent."

The following Sunday we were standing at the front door

of our new home. It was a brick row-house in the middle of a street lined with mirror images of the same house. The cement sidewalk served as the front yard, and three cement steps were the front porch that led to the metal screen-door of the entryway. Inside that was a living room, a long narrow space with one window looking out onto the street. On the left was a staircase leading to the second floor, where two bedrooms opened out from either side of the landing. A bathroom faced the stairs.

The dining room was just beyond the staircase, immediately followed by the kitchen, which had a tiny window facing the backyard. A small entryway led from the kitchen to the back steps and a fenced-in yard the size of a postage stamp.

"There's a yard! Can I garden here, plant vegetables and flowers?" The open space made me think of our farm and the vegetable patch Momma tended. She always made sure to have fresh vegetables and herbs in close proximity to the kitchen. I'd scurry out to pick whatever Momma needed as she prepared meals inside. I especially liked to pluck the mint and basil; both left a scent on my hands that tickled my nose as I inhaled. It made me imagine what food Momma had planned for that night's dinner. But the mint always ended up in a cool drink the adults sipped while out on the porch.

"Of course, you can do whatever you want. Gardening'll be good. I'd like to have some homegrown vegetables with our meals. This place needs to be cleaned up. You can take care of those things."

I relied on the church ladies and Phyllis to help me with the house. Phyllis had offered to come by our apartment when we first met, but I didn't want her—or anyone, for that matter—to see how we lived. Ginny and the girls were the only people who had crossed the threshold of the apartment, and after a time I couldn't stand having even them see my life inside those walls. But the house was different. It wasn't grand, but it was much more inviting than our apartment. There was space to move around without bumping into a piece of furniture or another wall. The windows in the living room brought street-level light inside that lit up the floors, almost making the wood look smooth and hiding the discoloration and scratches. Every room had wallpaper. The design was a collection of faded flower patterns on an off-white background. In the front room the primary floral colors were blue, in the kitchen green, and in the bedrooms were pink and yellow. I ran my fingers over the torn edges of the seams, thinking that a little glue would make it look new again. I wanted to love that house, but it was never my home, not like the home where I grew up.

Phyllis and the church ladies descended upon our new home like a flock of birds feathering a nest. It was nerve-wracking watching them inspect every corner of the house, making sounds as they nodded their heads but not saying anything to me. I followed their gazes, trying to determine if they approved of our house or thought it was a sorry-looking place. After inspecting the backyard, they came back in and started chatting away.

"I have some pieces of furniture just sitting in our garage —a small sofa, chairs with comfortable cushions, and decorative pillows," Phyllis said. "I'll have one of the boys bring those over for the living room."

"And we have a large kitchen table we don't use any longer," said one of the other ladies. "It'll look good in your kitchen. There are six chairs that match too. I'll have my husband bring those this weekend."

Another added, "The folding chairs taking up space in our attic will work in your backyard for something to sit on while you're watching the children play."

"I'd better talk to Henry first," I said. "He may want us to live with things as they are until we can buy furniture." But I began to imagine how different the house would look with more and better things sharing the space with us.

"Don't worry about Henry," Phyllis said. "I'll have my husband speak to him, tell him it's important for the church ladies to do what needs doing. You should let him know about our plans."

That night I made Henry's favorite meal. The house smelled as delicious as I knew the meatloaf would taste. While he was deep into enjoying his dinner, I said, "Phyllis and the ladies were here today. They liked the house and had suggestions on how I can decorate. They even offered to bring furniture, pieces that'll fill in the empty spots. They'll have it brought over this weekend."

"Don't want other people's furniture," he grunted.

"It was smart of you to work out a deal with your buddy for us to rent this place. Phyllis was very impressed—she said she'd talk to the Reverend about how you've done well by your family and how the church ladies would like to help out. We could invite the Reverend over to see our home, once it's presentable."

"She was impressed?"

"Yes, they all were—said this is a good neighborhood, close to church, and the house is one of the best on the block. It just needs some freshening. And we do need furniture. Is it okay to let them bring a few pieces? Once we buy our own, we can give it back or share it with someone else."

He grew quiet and kept eating the meal. I helped the children and anxiously waited for Henry to respond.

"She's talking to the Reverend about our house?" he asked.

"Said she would, probably tonight."

He finished his supper and got up to clean his shoes. One of the first things he'd done when we moved into the house was to set up a corner by the back door for his shoe-cleaning materials. There were several shallow shelves behind the door that had probably been used to store jars at one time. The tins of shoe polish, brushes, and rags fit neatly on the shelves. Henry had cleaned the area meticulously before placing his things there and standing back to admire the collection of items.

Now, as he was buffing one of his shoes, he said, "They can bring the furniture, but don't go behind my back again. Understand?"

"Yes, Henry," I replied.

"And I want to invite the Reverend over soon, so make sure everything looks good."

They showed up early Saturday morning with two trucks and several cars full of furniture and other household items. Henry greeted Phyllis at the front door as though he were welcoming special guests to his private manor. She brushed past him as if he weren't even there.

⌒ꟾ

I WAS HALFWAY through *Lady Chatterley's Lover* before the children's stirring caught my attention. I tore myself away from Constance and Oliver's lives to reenter my own and begin the everyday tasks that occupied my time and sensibilities as a wife and mother. I felt as though I should take a shower to help me regain control and make it easier to attend to the children, but I didn't want to wash away the lover's heat from my body or consciousness.

Wednesday night couldn't come fast enough for me. I'd finished the book by Saturday and hoped to speak to Charles on Sunday, but that didn't happen. He ignored me. I tried to get his attention when he sat in the pew across the aisle from where I was sitting with Henry and the children, but he looked the other way. He didn't offer to help in the kitchen either. Every time the door swung open I turned, expecting to see him stride in with a warm smile and offer to help. But he stayed away.

Phyllis asked, "You seem distracted—what's wrong, Nell?"

"Nothing, just have things on my mind," I said.

"Is everything all right at home?"

"Yes."

"And Henry?"

"You know how it is."

"By the way, Charles won't be in the kitchen any more. I told him we'd be just fine without the extra hands. Seemed like he was glad to go straight home."

I had to wait until Wednesday to let Charles know how much I'd enjoyed *Lady Chatterley's Lover*, how pleased I was that he wanted to share this particular story with me, and how my nights had become restless with thoughts of a love as profound as theirs. I paced the kitchen and the children's room of the church, waiting for him to arrive. After a while I sat in one of the chairs in the kitchen, then moved to the little children's chairs, then tried the overstuffed chairs in the sitting area just outside the main meeting space. I jumped up when I heard Charles say, "Hello, Nell."

"Hi," I replied. "I was deciding on the best place to sit."

"Come with me. I think the children's room is cozy." He took my hand and led me to one of the low tables that I used when reading to the children. He guided me into a chair and then positioned himself in one facing me. His legs straddled my knees, which were pressed together. He leaned forward, brushed a wisp of hair away from my right eye, and said, "Did you enjoy the book?"

"Yes."

"Are you blushing?"

"No," I said. But I could feel heat stinging my cheeks and looked away.

He lifted my chin and said, "It's a beautiful story. Did you know at one time the book was banned in England? It was considered obscene because of the explicit love scenes. The publisher was even sued, but they won the case, which propelled the book to record sales around the world. Most people think the story is only about great sex, but it's about much more than that. It explores class issues and marriage and relationships. All the things men and women face. But I must admit the sex scenes are amazing. Did you find the scenes—engrossing?" He traced my chin with his finger, then continued traveling down the center of my neck to the soft spot between my collar bones. My body trembled as Charles made circular motions, moved to the other side of my jaw, and placed his palm on my cheek. I rested my face against his soft hand and let him brush my lips with his thumb.

"You're lovely, Nell. Would you like to be my Lady?"

"Charles, I . . ."

"Shush, don't say anything." He stood and hovered over me, his legs still astride mine. Then he bent and kissed on my forehead. "I have to go."

"But we just got here," I said.

"I have things I need to do. But I'll see you next Wednesday."

I watched as he strode away and was aware of the rising and falling of my chest, the sound of my heart beating erratically, and the beads of sweat on my nose.

HENRY PACED THE kitchen. "What's wrong with you? Don't you hear the babies crying?"

He wanted me to stop cooking and take care of the children while he cleaned his shoes, but I didn't hear them, not the way I usually do. My mind wandered back to the look in Charles's eyes, the musky smell on his shirt collar, the sensation of his hands stroking my face, the feeling that something in my body was awakening. I didn't want to lose the images that caused my breathing to race and made me remember what it felt like to dream about loving a man the way I had when Henry and I first met. But I wondered what it would be like to be Charles's Lady.

"I was just thinking about church."

"You need to be thinking about your family. How long before supper is ready?"

"If I stop, it'll take longer to finish cooking. Why don't you look after your children?"

"That's your job."

I turned the heat down under the pots and went over to the children. Teddy needed a clean diaper, and Junior and April were tussling over a toy. I took care of their needs and finished preparing supper, but my mind was elsewhere.

Once the children were down for the night, I joined Henry in bed. He pretended to be asleep. I slid to his side and curled against his back, rubbed my legs against his, draped my arm around his waist, and reached for his private parts. He grasped my hand and pushed it away.

"Just thought we could have some loving," I said.

"Not doing that for a while, I told you."

"But . . ."

"Go to sleep. I need my rest."

I rolled over so that there was ample space between our bodies. Sleep came, and with it images on the insides of my eyelids began to form. Charles and I were in a field of wheat and wildflowers on a warm spring day. Birds were chirping, and a gentle breeze rustled through the grasses that provided harmonious background sounds for the singing birds. Charles reached for me and pulled me against him. He wrapped his arms around me. I leaned back and stretched, rested my head against his shoulder, encircled his arms with mine. The sun felt warm on my face as his lips moved up and down my neck. Suddenly we were on the ground, our bodies lost in the tall grasses that tickled my back and the exposed flesh of my thighs. He gently pushed my dress up around my waist. I held his face in my hands, tried to control my heavy breathing. My body was tense and arched with anticipation . . .

"Stop thrashing around," Henry grunted. "You sick or something?"

His voice shocked me back to my life. "Just feeling unsettled," I said, shaking the reverie away.

"Take something so I can sleep."

I got out of bed, pulled at the damp nightgown stuck to my chest and legs, and staggered to the bathroom. Resting against the sink, I stared at myself in the mirror. My legs were weak, and my dark skin had taken on a pinkish glow.

# Chapter Seventeen

"I THINK I'M IN LOVE," I BLURTED OUT AS SOON AS Charles took me in his arms and placed a gentle kiss on my lips.

Over the past month, Henry had gotten used to me leaving the house on Wednesday evenings. He'd actually accepted it, as though he realized it would give him a moment without me in the house. Soon it became a routine, with little need for us to discuss the whys of it. I'd just leave right after dinner, a free woman fleeing to another life. Once in the church kitchen, Charles and I would sit close to one another, touch, stare into each other's eyes. During each visit the touching became more and more intimate. His hands explored every inch of my body, and I learned about all of his muscles and his manhood.

"What do you mean?" Charles said as he ran his hands down my back, under my dress, tickling the soft insides of my thighs.

"You're in my head all the time, Charles. If I'm walking with the children, cooking, or cleaning the house, I'm tripping over images of you. The sound of your voice echoes through my head like a cool breeze on a hot day. I'm restless at night with thoughts of you. I lie down beside Henry, but my body betrays the feelings stirring for you. Henry's beginning to wonder what's wrong with me."

"We're just visiting, Nell, enjoying each other's company, sharing stories about what we read. No harm in that." He rubbed my shoulders. I closed my eyes and let the warmth from his hands soothe the questions stirring my soul.

"Is that all this is for you? Reading and talking?" I asked.

He took my hands and gently kissed one palm and then the other. I moved my upturned hand and stroked his cheek. His lips moved down my wrist to the inside of my elbow and then my face, where he lingered. He whispered, "The time we spend together is more special to me than the morning sun, more sensuous than a gentle rain brushing against a springtime bud, teasing it to full bloom. I cherish every second we have together. From the moment I met you, I knew that being near you was important for my soul."

He pulled me close. Our lips locked, moist and hungry. His tongue searched my mouth. I began to float, as though the dream-state from the night before had entered this space with us. Just as I felt myself give in to the ecstasy, I pushed Charles away and said, "I need some water." Then I made my way to the kitchen sink, where I stood just as I had last night in the bathroom, trying to slow my breathing and stop my heart from racing.

"Nell, I need to hold you. All this meeting, talking about books, sharing our deepest thoughts, and touching—I want to be closer to you." His body was within inches of mine, but I didn't turn around. He didn't touch me.

"This is wrong. We both know that." My words lived in one place, but my body was in another, and I eased back against his chest, closing the physical gap between us. My hands went from gripping the side of the sink to the fabric of my dress, then to the cloth of his pants. I dug my fingers into his thighs, felt his manhood grow, guided his hands to my breasts. My mind kept wanting to interrupt, to stop me and flee. But my body melted deeper and deeper against him.

"Just once, Nell. I want to make love and truly feel you." He began kissing the back of my neck.

The coolness of the large stainless-steel countertop heated up quickly from the temperature of our bodies pressed against the surface. Pots crashed to the floor. Water drenched us when we pushed against the faucet. We fell, and I bumped my head against the side of the cabinet.

"Are you all right?" Charles breathlessly asked.

"Yes, don't stop."

Spent, we sat on the floor in a puddle of water, our chests rising up and down in unison. I thought about my family, Phyllis's words of warning, nights of not being touched, and I almost felt ashamed. Then Charles kissed my exposed breast, and I stroked him; we rolled on the floor in a twisted knot. I cuddled against his chest, dozing on and off, reveling in my new-found feeling of euphoria.

"I have to tell you something," Charles whispered.

"I've never felt this—luxurious. Yes, that's how I feel right now," I said.

"I need to say something," he said. I could feel his body stiffen.

"What is it?"

"Nell, I'm leaving."

"I need to go too. But I don't want to move from this position."

"You don't understand. I'm leaving, moving away," he said.

I sat up, buttoned the front of my dress, pushed the hem down over my legs. "What're you saying?"

"This is my last night here. I'm going back to school. Now that everything is settled with my family, I need to get my life back on track."

I scurried away from him on my bum, like a small child escaping from danger. I grabbed my panties and frantically pulled them up my legs. He reached for me, but I slapped his hand away. "What have you done!" I shouted.

"Nell, I wanted one last special moment with you."

"Get away from me!" I screamed. A guttural sound flew out of me that was so loud it seemed to make the walls vibrate, sending the noise up the stairs to the altar.

"We both wanted this. Now we'll always have something to remember each other by." He stood, gathered his things to head out, and said, "You take care, Nell." With that he was gone.

"YOU PUTTING ON weight?" Henry asked one morning, weeks later.

The dish I was holding shattered on the kitchen floor. I told the children to keep their feet off the floor while I cleaned up the mess of broken glass. *What have I done?* I thought. *What have I done?*

"No, don't think so," I said. But I quickly turned my back to him and continued cleaning.

He walked into our bedroom while I was dressing. Long ago he had stopped watching me lotion my body, pull my underthings on, help me with a zipper or buttons running down the back of a dress. I was looking at my profile in the mirror—the growing bulge in my stomach and the full, rounder breasts—thinking about Charles and our love-child.

Suddenly Henry rushed at me, grabbed me by the shoulders. His grip was so tight it felt as though my shoulders were about to pop out of their sockets. "What—have—you—done?" he hissed at me.

"Henry—I—"

"Get rid of it."

"I can't, Henry, I just can't!"

"How dare you bring that into my home, to live among my children!"

"Henry!"

"You listen to me." He bent down and yanked my hair, bringing my face within inches of his. "You don't want to get rid of it—fine. You carry it for as long as you can, until the miscarriage happens. You tell everyone how we decided to have another baby. And when you get sick, you're on your own. You hear me? You'll be on your own."

He pushed my head to the floor and turned his back to me.

THERE WASN'T A particular day when everyone understood the baby wasn't Henry's. "We decided to have one more, before I'm too old—we want another girl," I said over and over, once my belly was too large for me to wear regular clothes. That was what Henry made me say, except the baby-girl part; that was my addition. I figured this time I could say what I wanted. But I could never make eye contact when I spoke that sentence; I could only look down at the tips of my shoes, the way I'd seen Daddy do years ago in the store. Most people found my reaction odd. They couldn't figure out why Henry and I didn't look happy about another child coming into the world. Henry had made such a commotion when Teddy was born. "My son, another son!" he'd pronounced to the congregation and run from man to man, grabbing their hands and slapping each one on the shoulder. His face shone with pride. But not this time.

However, there was a specific moment when the entire congregation knew that the life growing inside of me belonged to Charles. I thought I was alone in the children's room, where I'd escaped from the sermon that was making my head spin and my stomach churn. The Reverend was preaching about the virtue of honesty, how all of life's ills could be avoided if we all lived according to the moral standard of the Ten Commandments. He especially referenced the one about not committing adultery. Henry looked at me over the heads of the children, who were positioned between us in the pew. My cheeks stung so badly I had to get up and excuse myself. "Need the bathroom," I mouthed to him, and left.

I leaned against the wall to ease the lower-back pain that lived there daily and rubbed my stomach in circular motions. I began to imagine how beautiful this baby would be; somehow I knew it was a girl. Just the thought of her made me smile and think about Charles. "I want you to know about your daddy. But he'd probably want you to call him Dad—it's more Northern. He's an educated man, tall and handsome. He's a reader like me. We spent time talking about books, and you'll be a reader too. He had to go away, but I know he'll love you with all of his heart."

Suddenly I heard a gasp. There in the doorway was Phyllis. She glared at me, examined my face, ran her eyes down the length of my body, raised them back to my eyes, and held her hand in my face, like a crossing guard stopping traffic for school children. I opened my mouth to speak, but she shook her hand and said "No!" between clenched teeth.

"But—" I said.

She didn't blink, just moved her head from side to side, then abruptly turned her back, the way a disgusted actress would while breaking up with an unfaithful lover, and walked away.

## Chapter Eighteen

I DON'T REMEMBER HOW I GOT TO THE HOSPITAL. One day pain gripped my insides, and I gave in to the anguish as if hoping it was the signal of an end to the terror my life had become.

Once there I imagined Henry standing over me, wiping my forehead with a towel, moistening my lips with a wet sponge, and whispering, "I need you." Or was it Charles's voice? Silky and faraway, coaxing me back to reality. His lips brushing against my steaming hot forehead, his fingers stroking my cheeks, his manhood stirring inside me.

Then I felt the nurse trying to wake me. "You need to take some water and swallow these pills."

"My skin hurts. Don't touch me," I protested.

"You're going to be all right," she said.

For an instant I could see Henry standing in the doorway. Then my eyelids fluttered, and I imagined Charles kissing me, brushing my hair, wiping sweat from my forehead, and staring into my eyes. Was it Junior lifting Teddy so he could reach me to place a kiss on my cheek and wrap his arms around my neck? Or was it April who wanted to linger by my side? Did Junior push the other children toward the door? What was Momma doing here, and why did she look away from me? Why was Daddy shaking his head? The sheets felt cold and clammy around my legs as I twisted and turned on the unfamiliar mattress.

"I love you all," I said. "I love you."

My head kept spinning as though hot Louisiana heat were consuming me. I had visions—livestock milling around a barn that reeked of waste and rotten food, dust kicked up from arid fields as Daddy slowly took stock of what would no longer grow. My brothers' wives grieved the lives that weren't to be. Nieces and nephews, foreigners to me, squatted on the front steps, thankful for the reprieve from fieldwork, anxious about how much food would be on the table for dinner. My momma worked in the kitchen, pretending not to notice the devastation of her universe. The fields shimmered with hot emptiness.

Sudden cold enveloped me—I was freezing in a lonely house with no heat or hot water, in the dead of winter, frozen in a marriage bed where only sheets and blankets felt the touch of human flesh, chilled from the knowing eyes of a child watching, the coldness of unbearable shame.

Between my fits of unconsciousness I begged Henry for forgiveness. I called for Charles while clutching a gift from Teddy, my prized perennial from the backyard garden. The lily should have been beautiful; this was its time to be in full bloom, welcoming the world with its soft elegant petals, rich pink color, and delicately dusted interior stems. But it was handed to a mother wild with fever. It decayed before its time.

The doctors said I needed at least a week in the hospital. Baby Lilly was premature, and I was sickly. Henry begrudgingly brought the children to visit me. He sat in the car or the lobby, waiting for their visits to end. Teddy always asked, "Why isn't Daddy with us?" Teddy wanted to see Lilly during the visits. But I didn't want the children to see her in the little container with tubes attached to her mouth and nose. Teddy clung by my side and held my hand. The other children kept their distance. They huddled at the foot of my bed until it was time to leave.

The nurses took turns rolling Lilly into my room for me to bond with her. And then came days, once I was strong enough, when I'd make my way to intensive care and sit by Lilly's assigned tube, watching her breathe, reaching my hand inside and touching her, or blowing into the hole so she could feel my breath gently glide against her skin. Her fingers and toes curled as I touched her forehead. Lilly was a little dollop of an infant, barely bigger than a small sack of lemons in the produce section of the supermarket. She never made a sound, as though she instinctively knew her presence wasn't welcomed in the universe. One of the nurses told me that babies feel better when their mothers talk or sing to them. But I didn't know what to say to her. I hummed a church hymn and kept stroking her body.

"Hello, Nell."

I spun around when I heard his voice. "Charles!" I wanted to rush to him and wrap my arms around his body, to feel him against my chest. But then I thought about how he'd left me. I turned my back and said, "This is our child."

"I know. Phyllis told me."

"Why're you here?"

"I needed to see you."

"Why! You think I need more pain?"

"I'm sorry, Nell. I didn't want to hurt you."

"But you did."

"Phyllis thought it was best for me to leave. She could see we were too involved with each other; she knew there couldn't be a good outcome. So she pulled me aside one day and said it'd be best for everyone if I left you alone. I didn't want to, Nell. But she was right."

"You didn't just leave. You took what you wanted first."

"I'm sorry. I should've controlled myself, I know. But . . . I've missed you. My insides ache to be near you. I think about you all the time. From the first moment I saw you, my heart began to sing. I love you, Nell. But I didn't have that right, still don't. Still, once I heard about the baby I knew what I had to do. Taking care of our child is my responsibility, and so is taking care of you. That's why I'm here. Will you let me?"

"Let you? I don't know what that means. Look at her. She's barely alive, sucking air that's bumped into her tiny body. Torturous anguish courses through me every second because of what I've done and what it'll mean for this little one and the other children. Our love, if that's what it is, is too fraught with pain."

He pulled up a chair and sat close to me. Leaning against my back, he reached into Lilly's incubator to rub her hand. She twitched and gurgled in response.

"You'll see, Nell, I will care for you and our child," he said before he left.

After that day I let hope build a little flame inside my soul. It was just a tiny ember, like the tip of a cigarette after the smoker has taken the last drag and the filter is the only thing left to signal that the whole cigarette once existed. I had a lot of time to think while I healed in the hospital. In between the children's visits, time with Lilly, and interruptions by the nurses, which always seemed to happen just at the moment I dozed off, all I did was think about the mess my life had become. How could I ever explain all of this to Momma? I hadn't written to her in a long time. What would I say? "Dear Momma, I made a terrible mistake, and now you have another grandbaby, but the blood running through her veins does not belong to Henry."

When the tubes were finally removed from Lilly's mouth and nose, when the nurses said it would be all right for her to begin life outside of her plastic capsule, they brought her to my room in a crib, so I could take care of her until we were both ready to leave. I would have stayed right there in the hospital room until Lilly was a grown woman, if they'd let me.

Teddy wanted to hold Lilly during his next visit, but he was too young and she too little. I let him sit beside me on the bed instead, while I nestled Lilly on my chest and he held onto her arm. The other children clustered at the foot of the bed and watched as though they were the audience of a short movie unfolding before their eyes. I wanted Junior and April to touch Lilly and hug me, but they weren't interested. As soon as visiting time was over, they dashed out the door looking for Henry, while Teddy lingered on the bed until we heard Henry holler, "Teddy, let's go."

In my alone time, I kept hearing Charles's voice at the door. But he never visited me again.

We went home on a Wednesday. It had taken three weeks for me to recover from the difficult birth, for the fever to completely subside, for me to regain my strength and hold my head up on my own. The nurse wheeled Lilly and me to the outside door, and a cab driver helped us into his taxi. "Don't you have any family, Miss?" he asked. "What with a new baby and all."

"I want to surprise everyone."

We rode in silence. When we arrived at the house, it was empty. The children were in school, the youngest staying with friends, and Henry was at work. It didn't feel as though I were coming home but rather as though I were entering unknown territory in a foreign land, where I didn't have command of the language. I wanted to get my new baby girl settled in our home, but I wasn't sure how.

I reached out to Phyllis as soon as I got home. She'd been too busy to visit me in the hospital. "We won't be seeing much of one another any longer," she announced when I tried to strike up a phone conversation.

"But, Phyllis, I'll be in church. I'll see you and the other ladies there."

"Perhaps it'll be too difficult for you to attend church, what with such a large family."

"But . . ."

"Listen to me, Nell. I'm not saying I know exactly what happened, or if God would approve or disapprove of what you've done. It's not my place to make such judgments. And the fact is I'm not too happy with Henry either, so I'm not thinking about him—I struggle every day to find forgiveness for that man. As for Charles, well, frankly I thought better of him than this. But I am thinking about you. You may believe you're in love—maybe Charles said he loved you—but you have a husband. You need to ask the Lord for forgiveness. While God may forgive you, I'm not sure about the congregation. And you must figure out how you and Henry can continue to be together, given all of this. If you don't want to stay with Henry, then what? What about Junior, April, and Teddy? You've made a mess, Nell. I'll pray for you. Take care of yourself."

When Henry came home, I was in the kitchen, breast-feeding Lilly. He shouted, "Don't ever do that where I have to see it! Get out of my sight." I went upstairs to the bathroom.

The next day when Henry came home from work, he said, "You have to leave."

"What?"

"I can't look at you or it. You have to leave," he said again.

"Henry, I have no place to go."

"Phyllis'll be here soon. She's made arrangements." He sat down to clean his shoes.

A car stopped in front of the house. Phyllis, another church lady, and a woman I didn't recognize walked to the door.

Henry let them in and said, "Her things are over there." I hadn't noticed the two suitcases in the living room.

"Phyllis, what's going on?" I asked.

"Nell, you have to come with us. We have a place for you."

"I don't need a place. This is my home."

"Not any longer!" Henry shouted.

I turned to Phyllis. "It's for the best. Let's go," she said.

"No!" I screamed, and backed away from the door.

Henry grabbed my arm and shoved me. "Get out," he said.

"Henry, I'm sorry. I don't want to leave," I begged him. "This is my home. My children need me."

"Too late for sorry. I can't live with you," he barked back.

"What about the children—who'll care for them?"

"I've made arrangements. The church ladies'll help— Phyllis worked it out."

"Phyllis, how could you?" I screamed into her face. "I thought you were my friend."

"It's better this way, Nell, for everyone. You may not see it, but I'm being a good friend right now." Phyllis looked from Henry to me.

"This can't be happening. Where do I go?"

"To my home," the third woman said. "I'm Charles's mother, Catherine. I live all alone since my husband of forty years died and Charles moved out to finish his studies. I have a nice room for you and the baby, my grandchild."

She held out her hands to take Lilly from me, but I pulled away. "No!" I shouted.

"Nell, this is what Charles arranged," Phyllis whispered to me, with her back to Henry. "He convinced his mother to open her home to you. You'll be safe there, and Lilly will be loved. Given the situation, it's best."

I stared at her and saw the same fear in her eyes that I'd been holding in my belly since I walked into the house from the hospital. "The other children?" I asked.

"I'll make sure you see them on a regular basis. We need to go *now*," Phyllis said with urgency in her voice.

I looked over my shoulder at Henry, who was absorbed in polishing his shoes. My head was spinning. There were things I needed to do — prepare dinner for the children, pick ripe vegetables from the garden before they died on the vine, clean up the kitchen, fold clothes I'd left on the kitchen table, iron Henry's shirts for work and church. Phyllis tugged me. The screen-door banged shut as we walked down the steps to the car.

Lilly was nestled in my lap, wrapped in the pink blanket from her crib. My throat tightened when she looked at me with the same accepting expression on her face that she'd worn since the day she was born. An emptiness began to settle in my chest. It felt like a heavy vice squeezing my heart. Our reflection in the car's window was mixed with the city streets as we passed from the thickly settled, inner-city communities to the beginnings of the black suburbs, nestled just before the boundary of the all-white area. I thought about the bus ride, years ago now, with Henry. I'd been full of excitement and anticipation then, setting out on my first adventure, not sure of what would happen but content that I'd have a life as interesting as the characters in my books. The face that looked back at me today was not who I'd thought would emerge.

I began to wonder what Henry would say to the other children. As if reading my mind Phyllis said over her shoulder, "He told Junior, April, and Teddy that you're not well. You and Lilly need special care for a while."

"I don't know if I should thank you or hate you," I mumbled, more to myself than to her. "You can decide to hate me if that's what you need to do. One day you will thank me." We rode in silence until Catherine pulled into the driveway of the house that would become my sanctuary.

Once inside, Phyllis dropped my bags in the hallway and said, "I'll be praying for you." She turned and left me standing there with Charles's mother.

"I know this must be unsettling for you," Catherine said.

"It is for me too. But Charles convinced me that knowing my grandchild was important, in spite of the circumstances."

"When will he be here?" I asked.

"There are some things we need to discuss," she replied. "Let's sit in the living room."

"When will I see Charles?"

"Nell, you won't be seeing Charles. That's what we need to talk about."

"I don't understand."

"When I agreed to accept what happened and open my home to you, I did so with stipulations that Charles agreed to."

"Stipulations?"

"I want my son to have a full life, to finish his studies and begin his professional career as a lawyer. It'll take work and focus. I don't want him distracted. The agreement is that he will stay away from you and Lilly. You can live here and be safe, I'll get to know my grandchild, and when he's gotten his law degree, then he can decide on the next steps. But until then, I won't let him give up his life because of an affair."

"But . . ."

"You can accept these terms or go back to your husband. Now I'd like to hold my grandchild." She reached to take Lilly out of my arms.

I pulled away and backed against the wall.

"You have to decide, Nell," Catherine said with a steely look in her eyes.

Suddenly it felt as though I were hovering above the room, looking down at myself, Catherine, and Lilly. In an out-of-body state, I watched the scene like an interloper and saw the young mother's arms unfurl and Lilly slide from her to Catherine. The woman's eyes followed the grandmother as she walked away with Lilly and said over her shoulder, "Your room is up the stairs to the left. Take your things there." I continued to gaze at the figure below, which was me but couldn't be me, as she slowly pulled herself up the stairs and stood in the room that was to be her new home.

Another time, with a different set of eyes, I would have admired everything about the house and my bedroom. No black families I knew lived in homes with spacious rooms, large curtained windows, thick furniture covered in elegant pillows. But all I could see at the moment were my empty arms. In time I'd learn to appreciate these new surroundings; I'd come to understand that Phyllis had indeed been a good friend, that she'd probably saved my life, that Catherine's decision to open her home to me was an important turning point in spite of her stipulations concerning Charles, that the woman I'd eventually become was being formed in that bedroom the day I realized I'd lost my family. In the distance I could hear Catherine talking to Lilly in the baby sounds adults make to little ones. I couldn't acknowledge it then, but now I realize that those were sounds of a grandmother's love.

A phone rang somewhere downstairs. Catherine spoke in a hushed voice for a few minutes and then called up to me. "Nell, it's for you."

At the bottom of the stairs I found Catherine holding Lilly. She pointed to a small table in the alcove beneath the staircase where the phone receiver rested on its side.

"Who is it?" I asked.

"Your mother."

I froze.

"Nell, don't keep her waiting." Catherine held the phone out to me.

I stared at it as if it were a deadly creature being handed to me. With trembling hands I took the phone from Catherine and held it to my ear. "Momma," I said. "Is that you?"

"Baby Girl, it's me."

"Momma, I'm sorry." Tightness choked my chest; my legs became weak. I fell into the chair by the phone table and rocked back and forth, repeating over and over, "I'm sorry."

"Hush," Momma said. "Listen to me. Henry phoned to tell me what happened. The nerve of that man! To think for a moment I'd turn on my Baby Girl for him. I'm not happy about what you've done. But you my child, and I'll always love you and be there for you. Do you understand?"

"Yes," I said between gasps for breath.

"And I intend to know my new grandchild, so don't even think about keeping her away from me. Understand?"

"Yes, ma'am."

"This woman, Catherine, she's the man's mother? And she's looking after you and Lilly? Are you safe there?"

"I think so."

"And what about him, the father?"

"Charles? I'm not allowed to see him. That's the agreement for me staying here."

"And the other children? Where're they?"

"With Henry. Phyllis will bring them to visit once a week. At least for now."

"You need to gather all of my grandbabies and keep them with you."

"I don't know how, Momma. I have nothing. I'm so beholden to others. I've made a mess."

"Stop that whining! You think you're the first woman to make a mistake, the first woman to step out on her husband, the first to make a love-child? I know what that's about."

"Momma! What're you saying?"

"You never mind—just pull yourself together. There're things that need doing, and you're strong enough to handle it. You could come back home, but I'm guessing you don't want to live on the farm again. I've decided to send Robert to you. When he gets there, the two of you can figure out how to bring your family together. He can deal with Henry. You focus on the children. In times of trouble, a mother pulls her little ones around her and protects them like a collection of ducklings in the river. Now let's say a prayer for forgiveness."

With a bowed head I listened as Momma prayed. With every word she spoke to the Lord, a welcome calm spread throughout my body. We said "Amen" in unison, and then Momma said, "Let me speak with Catherine. Take care, Baby Girl, I love you."

"Love you too, Momma."

I handed the phone to Catherine. She listened to whatever Momma was telling her, but she didn't say anything in response, just nodded and stared at Lilly, who was fidgeting in her arms. Her expression changed during the ten minutes on the phone from that of a woman in charge of her home, who had begrudgingly opened her doors to an uninvited guest, to a woman taken aback by being put in her place by a stranger who lived a cultural lifetime away. When she hung up, she said, "Your mother is a smart woman. I look forward to meeting your older brother. Apparently he'll be here in two weeks."

I wanted to know what Momma had said to her. Catherine looked as though she were trying to absorb Momma's words and to decide how to view me in light of whatever she'd said. Momma wasn't one to speak in a stern voice to others. She was always gentle but subtle in her admonishment when she thought a child or adult had crossed her invisible line of acceptable behavior. She'd probably told Catherine about the importance of family. Even though Lilly had appeared in the world in less than desirable circumstances, Momma would want Catherine to appreciate the bond they had—two grandmothers charged with taking care of a new baby and mother. I was certain Momma had explained that she expected me to be safe, hence Robert being sent up North as soon as possible. I thought about something Daddy had said just before I left Louisiana after my wedding: "Remember, Baby Girl, you have family. No matter how far away you may travel, a person who has family is never alone."

I held Catherine's gaze as though we were two boxing opponents facing off before a title fight, until Lilly's needy baby sounds softened our intensity.

"I should give you a proper welcome and a tour of my home," Catherine said as she handed Lilly to me with a flourish, as if to emphasize that we'd be sharing her from now on.

I followed at her heels as she began to walk through each room of the house. She stopped at the fireplace in the living room to show me pictures of Charles from when he was a baby, from his military time, then college graduation photograph, and one of Charles with his father. Holding a picture of Charles in a football uniform, she said to Lilly, "This is your father."

# Chapter Nineteen

IT WAS SUNDAY AFTERNOON, AND I'D PREPARED A special dinner; I thought it was the least I could do for the kindness Catherine had shown me and the children. She'd invited me to make myself at home, after her conversation with Momma a week ago. When she left for church, I explored the kitchen to see what I could prepare. There I found all the fixings for fried chicken, greens, rice, and gravy. In the midst of cooking I began to think about Sundays in Momma's kitchen. It warmed my heart to remember the smell of cooking grease, fresh rolls in the oven, the sounds of little ones running out of the way of adults, and Momma giving her directions to everyone. At times it felt as if I were becoming Momma—as long as I didn't examine my current situation too closely.

In Catherine's kitchen cabinets I found her "good" dishes, the ones that were probably used on Sundays or special occasions. Hesitating, not wanting to overstep my welcome but wanting to make a good impression with the meal and table setting, I set the table with the delicate china. Matching serving bowls were in the lowboy cabinet in the dining room, along with a large serving platter. The crispy fried chicken looked delicious heaped onto the platter. My rice and collard greens overflowed in the bowls, which I placed on either side of the chicken. A gravy boat, with a silver ladle resting in its center, held my thick, tasty gravy. The aroma of a lovingly prepared meal hung in the air, just waiting for admirers.

When I heard the front door open, I expected to see Catherine and Phyllis with Junior, Teddy, and April, but when I walked to the entryway, there was Robert. I ran into his arms and drank in the fragrant aroma of our farm that was still clinging to his clothes.

"When'd you get here?" I asked.

"Last night, Sis."

"Where've you been—why didn't you come here right away?"

"There were some things needed to be done." Just then I realized that the children were with him, along with suitcases and boxes. "All the children will be staying with you from now on," he said.

"But what about Henry? What about Catherine? We can't all stay in her home."

"Yes, you may," Catherine said as she walked into the house. "I've given it some thought, after Robert and I had a chat. I could live alone in this big place and listen to myself rattle around, or I can open my arms and have a house full of family." She looked at the children and said, "You may call me Auntie."

"Robert, what did you say to Henry?" I asked.

"What needed saying," Robert replied. "There won't be any trouble from Henry. He gets to see the children when he wants, but they'll live with you. And if he gives you any problems, let me know right away."

Just like that, my world had taken another spin, as though it were a kaleidoscope, changing with every twist.

After dinner Robert and I sat in the living room on the big soft sofa with pillows overflowing along the back and sides. I squeezed his hand and said, "Tell me what happened."

"Not much to add, Sis. Momma said you needed help. I came as soon as I could. This is harvest time on the farm—I had to get as much done as I could before I left and make assignments for the others, to be certain we don't lose any crops. It's been a great growing season, and it'll be a good winter, with enough money to buy plenty of supplies to get us through the quiet farm time." He hesitated and squeezed my hand.

I looked around the room. While I admired everything in sight—from the family photos, to the thick floral curtains at the bay windows, to the small piano against the wall with a pretty oil painting of a field of flowers above it, to the tall floor-lamps with silk shades—it wasn't mine. I felt as if I were in a museum, moving around furnishings that were meant to be viewed by a visitor. I couldn't get a true sense of Charles in the house either, although I'd tried. The first time Catherine had left me alone in the house, I'd wandered to Charles's room. It still looked the way it had when he'd lived in it as a teenager still in school. Posters of athletes and musicians decorated the walls. His dresser was covered with trophies and ribbons for sports and academic awards he'd received. Baseball bats, gloves, a softball, and a basketball rested in a box at the foot of the bed. But there wasn't the scent of him that I longed for.

Finally I said, "Catherine is wonderful to welcome my family, but this can't last. She'll grow tired of not having her home to herself. And I'll grow tired of acting like I belong here but knowing in my heart that I don't. On the ride over here I thought about my bus trip with Henry. At the time it seemed like a grand adventure was unfolding and that all I had to do was sit back and enjoy myself. It was what I'd dreamed about—that once away from the farm I'd have experiences like the characters in my books. I never figured I'd end up being like Alice, tumbling down a twisted rabbit hole, struggling to live day by day."

"Not sure who Alice is," Robert said. "But why did things change with you and Henry? I thought you would be good together."

"I can't say there's just one reason we've ended up this way. Each day my dreams faded a little bit more, as though my eyesight were beginning to fail, until I couldn't recognize myself any longer. Suddenly Charles was there, and he stirred something in me that I'd feared was lost forever. . . . Are you ashamed of me?" That worry had been burning in my belly all day.

"Never ashamed of my little sis." Robert pulled me close and kissed me on the head. "I've seen love make people do foolish things before. You didn't write this book." He held me tight against his chest, and for the first time in weeks my body began to relax. "Charles seems like a good man," he said.

"You met him?"

"He lent a hand with Henry. Then he helped gather up the children and their belongings. He told me about the agreement with his mother. Can't say I blame her, but it must be hard for you and him to stay away from each other."

"I think about him all the time. We could talk for hours about almost anything, although we mostly talked about the stories in books. Sometimes he'd recite poetry to me, and I'd drift away listening to his soothing voice. It makes me sad that we can't see each other, but he's given me a gift in sharing his family's home with me and the children. I can live with the agreement—I don't have much choice. I've decided that getting a job is first on the list of what to do next. It's been a while since I saw my friends at the beauty shop, but Ginny may need some help. Maybe she'll take me back. And if not there, then maybe the library has a need for paid part-time help. I'll start looking as soon as the children are settled here and Catherine and I have worked out how we'll live together."

Robert cleared his throat and sat up straight. "I need to tell you something," he said. "Momma isn't doing well. You saw how she was when you visited a while back. She's gotten worse, in her head and in her body. The doctor's told us it won't be long . . ."

"No! Not Momma."

"She told me to tell you that your place is right here with *her* grandbabies; she thought you might want to come back with me once you heard this news. She doesn't want you traveling with them or leaving them here, what with everything."

"But I *should* move back and help Momma while I can. At least then the children and I would be in a home, a family home, not guests in someone else's."

"Sis, you need to stay here. Besides, you and the children are Northerners. You don't belong in the South."

"I wasn't there for Daddy, now Momma." I closed my eyes and could see her as though she were in the room. "Do you remember how at springtime she made us wash the kitchen walls? We'd turn it into a game, with more washing of us than the room. Then she'd scold us the rest of the day for making a mess."

"I was the one who had to clean up the mess you young ones made. If I complained, she'd tell me, 'Don't get sassy with me.' She always had us doing something to take care of the house and farm, saying, 'You think this place gonna take care of itself?' Those were good days."

"I hear her voice in my head all the time. The children will do something to try my patience, and it's her voice that comes out of my mouth, setting them straight. Sometimes I stand in front of the mirror, and it's her face looking back at me with soft knowing eyes. I'm not near her, but I feel like she's with me all the time. I don't want to lose her."

"In one way or another she's with us, just like Daddy. Your place is here with your children, Sis, the way Momma's place was with you."

We grew quiet and let silence paint images of our growing-up days. After a while I asked, "When are you leaving?"

"Tomorrow," he said.

"But you just got here."

"I did what I came to do, and now I have to get back. Here, these are for you." He handed me two envelopes. "This one's from Momma. Miss Parker helped her write the letter. And this one's from Charles."

I took the letters and turned them over to examine the handwriting. On the envelope from Momma were the words *Baby Girl*, written in crooked lines as though a child just learning cursive had picked up a pen to play at writing. On Charles' envelope the words *Nell My Love* appeared in elegant script, almost like the calligraphy in the old books I'd thumbed through in the library many years before.

I tucked both envelopes into the pocket of my skirt, knowing I needed solitude to savor the words from two people dear to my heart. I turned to Robert and said, "Thank you, for everything. I love you."

THREE DAYS PASSED after Robert left before I finally sat down to read my letters. At night, after putting the children to bed, I'd hold each envelope to my face for a whiff of the ink and paper, then gingerly place the letters on my nightstand. In the mornings I'd put the letters back into the pocket of whatever I was wearing for the day and occasionally tap them as I went about my daily activities, which mostly involved getting the children settled in Catherine's home. Although she was quick to correct me and say, "*Your* home."

"Junior and Teddy will have Charles' old room as theirs," Catherine had told me the day the children arrived. "April can join you and Lilly in your room." Robert had helped place a small bed in the room for April. At first I thought it would be too small for the three of us in one room. But then I remembered how we'd lived in a tiny apartment, just one room with a bathroom. This bedroom was twice the size of that space.

The best way I could think of to thank Catherine was to make sure the children stayed out her way, didn't make too much noise, and didn't leave their few toys anywhere in the house other than in their rooms. But on that first afternoon she introduced them to the TV room, as she called it, and told them that they could play there with any of their toys. I noticed her face light up whenever they called her Auntie.

This particular day Catherine had taken the children outside to explore the yard and neighborhood. "I'll take them to meet the neighbors," she said as they headed out the door. I watched her from the window. She looked like a proud aunt who wanted to show off her collection of little people. I think that was the first time I noticed how beautiful my children were. There's something about seeing your children through the lens of someone else's eyes that sheds new light on their countenances.

I chose the bedroom as the place where I'd settle into and finally read my letters. While both envelopes had been burning a hole in soul, Momma's words were the ones I needed to savor first:

*Dear Baby Girl,*

*I pray for you every day, knowing that you've found yourself in difficult times. My days may be short, but my love for you will be everlasting. I don't want you to come back to the farm when I join your daddy with the ancestors. There's no point in you traveling all the way here to look at my dead body or a mound in the ground alongside Daddy's. This place was never for you. And truth be told, there are times I didn't want it for me, but our lives were meant to be very different. When you left, I felt joy, knowing that you'd taken off on the adventure that had been tugging at your insides since you were five years old. You may have come from the farm, but you were never meant for the farm like the rest of us. We wear the dust, seed, animals, and hot air of this place like it's our second skin. For you it was just a covering meant to be removed at will, no more permanent than a hooded slicker on a rain-soaked day.*

*I'm not sure you need to hear this, but know that I forgive you. Something powerful must have forced you to turn away from Henry and to Charles. If you pray on it, God will forgive you too. Remember, the Lord is never going to give you more than you can bear. Nothing will ever take away the good memories you have of me, Daddy, your family, and the farm. You've been a wonderful daughter. Now I will join Daddy in watching you from above. I love you, and I'm also very proud of you.*

*Love,*
*Momma*

I crawled under the covers and buried my face in the pillow. The blankets felt like the heavy protective shield the dentist placed on my chest before x-rays. I couldn't move my arms or legs, couldn't lift my head, couldn't turn onto my side. I lay on my back and stared up at the ceiling. The blanket pressed harder, and my body ached. It felt as though I were disappearing into the center of the mattress, sinking into oblivion. I expected tears to run down my face, but my tear ducts were dry and parched.

Hours later I sensed Teddy at my side, saying, "Mommy, you need to get up." I moved to get out of bed. My body barely responded. I thought, *I should've been standing by now*, but the searing pain that ran from my toes to my head paralyzed me.

Suddenly I heard Momma's voice. She told me to be

strong, to stand and tend to my family. The rest of the day I did what needed doing—settled the children in their rooms after the neighborhood tour, worked with Catherine to prepare dinner, put the little ones to bed, and helped with the clean-up. Catherine kept the children occupied as she watched me moving around the house like a lost zombie. At one point she asked, "Are you all right?" I nodded, yes, and then went to my room.

Charles's letter was on the nightstand. After reading Momma's words, I wasn't certain I could handle what he had to say. In my heart I hoped that his words would be of enduring love and would give an indication of when we'd be able to hold each other, kiss, and rekindle our passion. I wanted him to tell me he'd be home soon. Slowly I reached for the envelope to take the folded paper out. After several deep breaths to ease the pain in my stomach, I began to read.

*Dear Nell,*

*I miss you. It's impossible to find the words that clearly describe the agony coursing through my mind each day that I'm away from you. When I saw you in the hospital and set eyes on our baby for the first time, I wanted to sweep you both up into my arms and flee to a world we could call our own. But I had to stand fast, knowing that my rights to anything about you and your life are constrained by the reality of who we are.*

*I love that you and Lilly are living with Mother. While her requirements for this arrangement aren't what I wanted, it's important to know that you're safe*

and as close to me as possible. When I come by the
house to take Mother to church, I beg you, come to
the window, draw back the curtains, let me see your
face so I can have one moment of joy. Mother is firm
in her beliefs of what's right and wrong. But I'm
confident that once she comes to know the woman
and mother you are, her edges will soften.

I'll pray for the day when you and I can stand in
the same space, touch one another, and become a
family—all six of us. Until then, please keep your love
for me as precious as I'll keep mine for you, and know
that I'm doing all I can to ensure that you and the
children will be well provided for. Maya Angelou
wrote, "In the flush of love's light, we dare be brave.
And suddenly we see that love costs all we are and
will ever be. Yet it is only love which sets us free . . ."

With all my love,
Charles

# Chapter Twenty

IT WAS MIDNIGHT, BUT SLEEP WOULDN'T NESTLE IN my mind. I twisted and turned in bed in a half-dream, half-awake state. Images of the places where I'd lived flowed through me, but with every turn it seemed that furniture was rearranged or missing. My childhood bedroom on the farm was empty save for the little dresser where my few pieces of clothing were neatly folded in drawers. The bed in the first apartment that Henry and I had shared was moved to the wall against the windows. It faced the bathroom, and the kitchen table was at the foot of the bed. In our rented house the back door was missing; there was no way to go out to the garden. My vegetables were rotting on the vine, with flies buzzing on the spoiled food. Only Catherine's house and the room I shared with my girls remained the same as the day I'd entered it.

I got up, went downstairs, and stood on the front porch. Evening light washed over my face, and cool air brushed the tiny hairs on my skin. The autumnal equinox was upon us. I'd come to love this time of year in New England, as the evening air turned crisp and yet the days were still warm and inviting. At times the harvest moon shone so bright that the house and yard would be illuminated as though it were the midday sun sending its rays down to earth. I closed my eyes and listened to the soft trembling of leaves clinging to trees as the wind moved in gentle swirls. Momma's voice seemed to whistle through the dancing branches.

"Momma," I said, "I pray you're not ashamed of me. I tried to do things the way you taught me—to be a good wife and mother. But none of your teachings prepared me for the loneliness of a marriage without love or a world bereft of family close by. Church was a welcome place for me, but not any longer. I've been shunned by the church women and made invisible. It's as though a blazing scarlet letter on my chest blinds them to my presence, and they turn away to protect their eyes. . . . I love Charles and refuse to feel sinful. . . . I miss you and Daddy."

Suddenly a warm breeze seemed to enter my body and touch every inch of me. The pleasant sensation eased my muscles. I went back to bed and welcomed a deep sleep.

Hours later the faint sound of the phone ringing downstairs woke me. I listened to Catherine's muffled voice through the floorboards. When she knocked on my door and said, "Nell, it's Robert," I knew Momma was gone.

"She went in her sleep," Robert told me. "She'd been feeling weak and dizzy at suppertime, went to bed early, and was gone in the morning."

"I could feel her last night, Robert—it was as though we visited. I can't believe we'll never see her again or hear her words of advice and wisdom."

"I have a box of things she wanted you to have. I'll ship it next week."

"What about the services?"

"She made all the arrangements for the funeral home to

handle the cremation and a memorial service at church. I'm merely following her instructions."

"I . . ."

"No, don't come. You know Momma didn't want you to."

"My children won't know her. They won't experience her cooking or her stories or her warmth. I should've stayed after Daddy died."

"Sis, stop. Your children have you. Honor her by giving them what she gave you."

When I hung up the phone, the churning in my stomach was overpowered by the throbbing behind my eyes. I went back to the bedroom and waited for grief to paralyze me or force me into a fetal position wracked with sobs. But I was numb and empty. Slowly I dressed and went down to find Catherine and the children. They each gave me a hug and then they nestled in the TV room, playing quietly. I thought about Robert's words but wondered how I'd ever be able to do for my children what Momma had done for us. She was the matriarch of a complete family unit, with traditions that we as children could count on every day. I was living in my lover's home with his mother, cast out by the church, unable to turn to Charles for comfort or companionship, and uncertain what would happen with Henry. I said to Catherine, "Do you mind watching the children? I need to walk a bit and get some air."

"Take all the time you need. I'm sorry about your mother." She gave me a hug.

*One foot in front of the other,* I thought as I left the house, not knowing where I'd go. *Keep moving. Let the air and forward motion push anguish away.*

I stopped in front of the public library and admired the

huge doors that had impressed me the first time I'd seen them, when Henry brought me there years before. Life is full of *firsts*, which cling to our memories like little pieces of floating stardust. Sitting on the park bench, I saw that young girl who had stood on those steps at the age of sixteen and marveled at her first experiences. Was the child bride who had held onto whatever Henry said, as though his thoughts and words came from a great novel, actually me? How had I become a twenty-two-year-old woman who was homeless and had just become a motherless child? When I remembered Henry dragging me down the steps of the library, I leapt from the bench and continued walking.

My pace quickened with each step, until I was almost jogging. Buildings and storefronts all became a blur as I aimlessly sped down the street. The tips of my shoes were the only things clear in my view. I hurriedly placed one foot in front of the other, one foot in front of the other. I bumped into people on the sidewalk but didn't stop. I pushed my way through groups of college kids, nearly knocking their books to the ground. I circled around mothers with strollers and forced couples walking hand in hand to step aside as I stormed through. I stepped off the curb but was jolted to a stop when a car horn blared. The driver shook his fist and pointed to the green light. A man who was waiting for the walk sign asked, "Are you all right?"

I backed onto the sidewalk. "Yes," I panted.

Once across the street I began walking at a slower pace and started to notice the neighborhood. Ginny's shop was on the block, a place where I'd found a sense of joy in another time of my life. I looked in the window and watched Ginny and the girls do what they'd been doing when I'd first met them. With deft hands they worked customers' hair and chatted away at the same time. The scene felt comforting, so much so that my breathing began to slow. But when Ginny turned and noticed me, I backed away on my heels and hurried down the street.

It was a welcome sight to see Catherine's house and the black mailbox with the red metal flag standing at attention. I leaned against the wrought-iron fence, wiped my pounding forehead, and wondered, where are the tears? News of Daddy's death had sent me howling in pain, unable to stop the flood of tears from drenching my body. But for Momma—none. It was as though my tear ducts were suffering from dry heaves, which hurt yet denied me emotional release.

I heard footsteps on the porch. Charles ran down the steps and said, "Nell!" He folded me in his arms, and it was then that the dam holding my tears hostage came loose. I sobbed into his chest. "I buried my Daddy . . . now Momma. . . . The children and I don't have a home!"

He lifted my chin and looked into my eyes. "Come inside," he said. "You'll always have a home here."

# Chapter Twenty-One

ROBERT WAS THE PERSON I WANTED TO CALL RIGHT away and share that Charles and I were getting married—not that there was anyone else for me to reach out to. "I'm happy for you, Sis," he said, on the new phone he'd had installed at the farm after Momma's passing. "I prayed to Daddy and Momma to ask for their blessings. I believe they're happy for me too."

"What about the children, Sis—will they stay with you?"

"Charles wants to adopt Junior, April, and Teddy. That way we'll be one family. I don't think Henry will object. For the first few weeks after I moved out, he'd come visit and take the three children for the day. Slowly that turned into a few hours once a week, then to every other week, and then to not at all. I think when Junior started to ask for new shoes and clothes, Henry decided he'd had enough. It broke Junior's heart not to hear from his daddy, and there wasn't anything I could say. Guilt clings to my heart where they're concerned. Charles tries to fill in the gaps, and he's come to love all three like they're his own, but blood is thicker than mud in the hog's pen. That's something Momma always said."

"I knew Charles was a good man. Junior'll come around, you'll see."

"How's the family?"

"Everyone's doing great. I'm making changes to the farm,

trying to move into the twentieth century, something Momma resisted. She always said, 'Leave good enough alone—things have worked all these years, it'll continue just fine.' But change was needed, and I'm enjoying making my own path."

"I finally opened the box you sent. The pictures of Daddy's and Momma's parents are on the mantelpiece alongside Charles's family pictures. It brings back warm memories of the farm and of the spots where the pictures were on the wall and at Momma's bedside. I can see her holding the picture of her parents and rubbing her finger over their faces before going to bed. I tell the children stories about their grand and great-grandparents, just the way we were told. . . . Can you be here for my wedding?"

"Sorry, Sis, but there's too much going on here. You have my blessings, and I hope y'all come visit us soon."

"I love you, Robert."

"Love you too. Bye."

I cradled the phone for a moment, thinking about Robert. I knew he would always be my big brother that I could count on any time for anything; but in the back of my mind there was a sorrowful sensation—I knew then that I'd never see the farm again.

ON SUNDAY CATHERINE and the children set off to church wearing the new clothes that Charles and I had bought for them, which I'd decided they'd also wear for our ceremony. I watched longingly as everyone waved good-bye to me and headed out. Charles said, "I'll speak to the Reverend about officiating our wedding."

"I think it's best if I talk to Phyllis. She and I still have rough edges between us that need smoothing," I responded.

He kissed me and left.

It comforted my heart to have Charles back in my life and to watch him develop a close relationship with the children. After Catherine had told him about Momma, she'd said that he needed to be here for me, and that she'd let go of the requirements for sharing her home. When I fell into his arms after my frantic walk, we went into the house and held each other as we'd done when we first met in the church kitchen. My body responded to the touch of his hand, the curl of his arms around my shoulders and waist, the scent of his hair, and the rising of his chest as my head pressed against him. We stood in the entryway, folded into one another, as if we were on a dance floor slowly swaying to a sensual jazz tune.

Nevertheless, although Catherine allowed him to come and see me, we still couldn't be with one another the way I wanted. "It'll take time," he said. I was beginning to lose patience, waiting for time to catch up to my needs.

At seven o'clock that evening I phoned Phyllis, knowing that Sunday supper would be over and the dinner guests on their way home. Her phone rang five times before I heard her voice and said, "Hello, Phyllis, this is Nell."

There was silence on the other end of the phone; I could almost hear thoughts of admonition in her breathing.

"I need to ask you something. Charles and I have decided to get married, and we'd like to have the Reverend officiate our wedding. It's going to be a small service, here in the living room with the children and Catherine and hopefully you as well."

I waited for her response, but there was only silence. Finally she said, "I'll think on it."

Two days later the doorbell rang. I looked out the window and saw Phyllis standing there with two other church ladies, Irene and Brenda. I never had liked Irene—she would bark orders at me in the church kitchen as if I were her servant. She'd sat in the back seat when Phyllis and Catherine had taken me from my old house here to Catherine's, wearing a scowl on her face for the entire ride. She never once looked me in the eye. Brenda, though, had helped me get comfortable in the church when I'd first arrived. She took the time to explain where everything was, how to handle the banquet-style pots, and how to manage cleanup in the bathtub-sized stainless-steel sink.

Today they looked like women who could have been on the cover of *Ebony* magazine. The long, thin pencil-skirts that each was wearing came to just below their knees, their high heels and pointed-toe shoes created a long and elegant look for their nylon-stocking-covered legs. They held gloves in their hands, and little purses dangled at the crease in their bent arms. They even had hats on, as if they were about to walk into church. I wasn't sure why Phyllis had felt the need to bring an audience with her just to tell me *no* about the wedding.

I opened the door after rubbing the creases in my house dress and running my fingers through my hair.

Phyllis said, "Hello, Nell. We'd like to visit if this is a good time."

"Please come in." I let them pass, and we walked into the living room.

"We won't be long—we don't even have time to sit," she said.

The four of us stood in the living room, rocking back and

forth on our heels. No one said anything, and they didn't look directly at me. Their eyes wandered around the room as though they had entered a museum and wanted to get their bearings.

After a few moments Phyllis said, "We discussed it and have come to a decision."

"Discussed what?" I asked.

"You and your behavior," Irene spit out, as if she had a sour taste in her mouth and needed to clear it away.

"Hold on, Irene," Phyllis said. "Nell, you need to realize that this is about more than you and Charles. When a woman of the church steps out on her husband, and with someone who is beloved by the congregation, it sends a cloud of tension over all of us. A church family is grounded in trust."

"We don't want to be looking over our shoulders to see who's eyeing our husbands!" Irene chimed in, giving me a look that could have stopped a tornado.

"How dare you come here and speak to me that way! What makes you think anyone would want your husband in the first place?" I shot back.

Phyllis touched Irene's arm and said, "We discussed this . . . be still." She turned back to me. "God is forgiving. We prayed on it and asked the Lord to show us the way to forgive you and welcome you back. It's not right for children to be in church without their mother, because worshiping the Lord is about family. But forgiveness is a long road that we've only just begun to walk down." She gave Irene a sideways glance.

"Oh Phyllis, that sounds like something my momma would say." I sighed.

"I'm sorry for your loss, Nell. . . . But will we see you in church next Sunday?"

"Church has always been an important part of my life. Not going has left a large void inside. I hope it'll be possible for me to join you in the kitchen again."

The women looked at each other. "Let's take one step at a time," Phyllis said.

"And my wedding?" I asked. "You'll come?"

"You need to be divorced first!" Irene hissed.

"Irene, why don't you and Brenda wait outside?" Phyllis snapped.

Irene spun around to the door with her right hand on her hip and sashayed away but looked over her shoulder and made a "humph" sound as the door closed.

"Nell, this isn't going to be easy. We're Godly women, but we *are* women, full of all the imperfections that come with being human. There's a part of me that can understand your actions—Henry's certainly no prize, and Charles is a treasure—but there's another part that recoils at what's happened. However, when I see Catherine in church with the children, watching how they've taken to her and the way she responds to them, I realize it's the little ones we need to think about."

"The children love Catherine; they call her Auntie. . . . Phyllis, I remember how you opened your arms to me the first time I showed up at church. I told you when we came to Catherine's that I wasn't sure if I should hate you or thank you. I do owe you a world of thanks—you may have saved my life." She patted my shoulders and said, "I'd be pleased to be at your wedding, and of course the Reverend will conduct the ceremony. But understand, when you come to church, at times it'll feel like you need to tip-toe before you can take firm steps."

# Chapter Twenty-Two

THIRTY DAYS AFTER OUR ATTORNEY SENT HENRY the divorce papers, he dropped them off at the house and told me he was going back South. "It'll be easier for me to be my own man there," he said. "I have a little something to start over with too." He didn't want custody of the children and told me Charles could have the adoption. "They's yours and Charles's children now." Anger seemed to have left his face for a moment. Then he said, "Nell, I did the best I could. "

My throat clamped tight and goose bumps began to crawl on my arms. I saw my reflection in his eyes of the child he had taken at sixteen years old and who he had tried to shape into what he wanted without any regard for me as a person. "It wasn't good enough," I said. "You imprisoned me and then pushed me out. What I did was wrong and I've asked forgiveness for my sin. But you stole my childhood!" My words were devoid of hate or anger; they floated on currents of resignation. "Do you want to see the children, at least Junior, and say good-bye?" I asked.

"No." He threw the papers at me and left.

I watched his back as he sauntered away. It made me think about the young man who'd sat on the steps with Daddy and the other men, waiting for me to make an appearance. I thought about the young girl-child who had been me at the time, anxious to learn and to please a new man in her life. With a sigh and a shake of my head to brush the past away, I closed the front door.

When I told Charles that night about what had happened with Henry, saying that I didn't understand his comment about being able to start over, Charles said, "I gave him money, Nell. It's what he demanded for signing the divorce and adoption papers. He won't be in our lives any longer."

## Chapter Twenty-Three

WE WENT TO THE COPLEY PLAZA HOTEL FOR OUR honeymoon. I didn't understand what it meant to "honeymoon" but Charles explained that it was customary for newlyweds to get away after the wedding to be alone and begin their life together. We weren't going to travel far because Charles had to prepare for the bar exam, but we'd take a few days at the hotel and plan a trip later. Honeymooning wasn't something I'd ever seen happen in the farmland of the south, but I liked the idea. Once we settled in our room, Charles took me in his arms and we danced to a slow tune that was playing on the radio.

"I've missed being with you, Nell." He kissed me and ran his hands over my body.

"I've missed you too," I said. We found our way to the four-poster bed that was covered in fluffy down-filled quilts and decorative pillows. It took just one kiss and the touch of his fingertips on my breast for heat to rise up, take hold of our bodies, and rekindle our passion.

We spent two days at the hotel and didn't leave the room until it was time to go home. When we checked out, the man at the front desk asked, "Did you enjoy your stay, Mr. and Mrs. Johnson?" I remember being startled to hear my new name.

"Yes, it was divine," I said and curled my hand around Charles' arm as he paid the bill. We stepped outside and Charles looked across the street at the library.

"Would you like to go in before we head home?" he asked.

I hesitated for a moment and replied, "Not today, let's go home."

Catherine and the children greeted us at the front door with hugs and kisses.

"I think I'll get changed and play with the children awhile," I said and headed upstairs to my room.

"I've had your things moved," Catherine said. "You and Charles will have the master bedroom now. I've moved into the room off the kitchen."

"I don't understand," I said looking from Catherine to Charles.

"Nell," Charles said. "They're some things we need to talk about."

I followed him into the study that had been his father's and that Charles had been using when he visited for quiet space to read. The children weren't allowed in the room and I'd only peeked into it on one or two occasions. It had an oversize intricately carved wood desk with a tall-back brown leather chair that was worn on the seat and arms. I'd admired the bookshelves that lined three of the walls of the room from floor to ceiling. There were so many books. I'd decided that one day I'd read every book there before I went back to the public library.

We sat facing each other in two chairs in front of the desk.

"I need to go over some family matters with you,"

Charles said. He took a folder off the desk that was filled with important looking papers. Daddy had a folder like that, although his was tattered and smeared with grease stains, not clean and smooth on the outside like this one. Sometimes he and Momma would sit at the table and talk about the papers as he'd turn each over in his hand. A serious look would cloud over their faces. It was as though they were engaged in life or death matters. Charles had that same look.

"Mom moved into the in-law suite off the kitchen. My parents had the addition to the house built a few years back in anticipation of my grandmother moving in with us. But that didn't happen. Now that we're married, Mom said she wanted to use the suite for herself so we can have the master bedroom. It's actually better, going up and down stairs is getting difficult for her. And besides. This is *our* house, yours and mine." He sat back and took a deep breath.

"My dad left everything to me when he died—this house, the contents in it, his car, bank accounts and stocks, our cottage on Martha's Vineyard."

"Martha's Vineyard?" I asked.

"It's an island off the coast, only a few hours from here. I grew up summering there, now the children will."

"An *island*, I've never seen an island, only read about them."

"We'll go this summer."

"But what about Catherine, if your father left you everything?"

"Mom's well taken of," he said.

Charles explained that there were several life insurance policies that named Catherine as the beneficiary and she had money from her family. The one obligation in his father's will was that she would live in the house until she died. He showed me all the legal papers and alongside his name as the owner on the houses and the car, was my name.

"We own all of this together," he said.

I knew it'd take time for me to absorb what Charles was saying, but there were matters on my mind too. I asked, "May I learn to drive, and get my high school degree? I want to apply for college and study to become a teacher. I'd like to get a job. May I do all of this?"

"Nell, you don't need my permission to live your life." He stood and took me in his arms and said, "I love you, let's go to our new bedroom, see if that bed is as comfortable as the hotel's."

# Chapter Twenty-Four

THE FAMILY AND I HUDDLED AROUND THE TELEVISION one summer day and watched images that were being broadcast from Mississippi of white policemen knocking down young black men and women, even children, with powerful fire hoses turned on full force. We watched mean dogs tearing at people's clothing. We saw the dogs' fangs pierce people's arms and legs drawing blood. We saw hate stamped across the faces of whites as they yelled obscenities and shouted racial slurs. Charles and Catherine gasped as the images continued, but I didn't. I was horrified too but not surprised by what was projected on the screen. For black southerners racism lived in the air we breathed. It had a face that we saw each day, it sounded like the hiss of a swarm of bees, and it smelled like the stench from the hog pen that never cleared from our nostrils. I'd learned that the north liked to hide its racism behind smiles and seemingly better living conditions. The broadcast from Mississippi brought the southern black experience to northerners' living rooms for the first time.

Catherine said, "Please turn the TV off, the children shouldn't see this."

"I want them to see; they need to know," Charles responded.

Catherine got up and went to her room.

I thought about the day in school, almost ten years ago, when Miss Parker showed us the picture of Emmet Till's beaten body. We were scared when we saw the brutality, but she said, "You children need to know."

In September the family and I watched another broadcast from Mississippi. This time it was images of a church that had been bombed by the Ku Klux Klan. Four young black girls were killed in the blast. In their pictures displayed on the screen it looked as though the girls were dressed up for church or school. Junior asked, "What happened, Daddy?"

Charles said, "A church was bombed, by mean people."

"The girls were inside?" April asked with a look of fear on her face.

"Yes, they were," I said.

"Why were they killed?" she wanted to know.

"Because those people don't like us," I replied.

"Why?" she asked, then added, "They look like me."

Charles and I glanced at each other with identical contemplative expressions on our faces that silently said, "How, where, do we begin?"

When we tucked the children in bed that night neither of us wanted to leave them alone. That was the first time I understood the rueful look and unexpected hug Momma had given me on the front porch of the farm the day Daddy and I came back from the store without any food.


WHENEVER PEOPLE HAD a disagreement with someone else Momma used to say, "Just be still with it and let time take over. Things change, people move away, sometimes they get sick, eventually they'll even pass on." She'd told her friend that when the friend complained about how she'd gotten fired by her missus because of the damaged lace. Momma's friend wasn't welcomed at the missus' funeral that took place months later, but she went anyway and stood in the shadows. "I had to see for myself, to be certain," she'd told Momma. I thought about Momma's saying when I stood with the congregation at Irene's funeral. I didn't have to hide in the shadows, but I did stand off to the side away from her family and close friends.

It'd taken a while for the church ladies to get comfortable with me being back, just as Phyllis had warned. I'd tip toed into church for services at first but eventually everyone embraced me along with the family—except for Irene. When I'd tried to work in the kitchen, she'd stood at the doorway like an imperial guard who had no intention of letting me pass. Phyllis and Brenda had caught my eye and shrugged and looked away. The kitchen was off limits as long as Irene was in charge and held onto her disdain for me. But one day she was filling a large pot with water at the sink and as she went to lift it she let out a piercing scream and grabbed hold of her chest and fell to the floor. Brenda was there; she retold the story. She called for help but Irene succumbed to the massive heart attack before the ambulance got her to the hospital.

I'd decided to wait two weeks after her funeral and then go back to the kitchen and ask Brenda and Phyllis if they needed my help. That morning I fidgeted with my clothes while getting dressed, I rushed the children into the car, and told Charles we had to get to church early.

"Why?," he asked.

"I plan to help in the kitchen, or at least see if the women will have me back. As soon as the service is over I'll head downstairs."

"You're sure about this? I mean, that's where it all began for us," he teased.

"I hadn't thought about it that way."

"I may show up there too." He reached for my waist and pulled me close.

"Stop, we have to go." But I didn't move away from him until our kissing had calmed me down.

*The longest sermon in the world*, kept running through my mind as the Reverend droned on and on. I didn't listen to anything he said or hear the choir's songs or remember singing hymns with the congregation. The children kept looking at me as if to say, *what's wrong?*, as I wiggled in the pew like they usually did. Charles took my hand and whispered, "Breathe."

When the Reverend finally gave us blessings for the day, I made my way to the stairs behind the pulpit before anyone else had left the pews and moved into the aisles to leave. At the bottom of the stairs I stopped and inhaled deeply to fill my lungs with air and then slowly let the air out through my mouth. Once at the kitchen door I watched Phyllis, Brenda, and the other women as they hurriedly moved about preparing the after-service meal the congregation enjoyed once a month. The aroma of collard greens and ham hocks simmering on the stove along with the heavy scent of sizzling fried chicken draining on paper towels made me close my eyes and delight in the redolence of food cooking in the church kitchen that I'd missed.

"Nell," Phyllis said. "Are you just going to stand there or do you intend to help?"

"Well," Brenda said, "Looks like Mother Nell is back. You know where everything is, make yourself right at home."

CHARLES HAD GRADUATED with honors from law school and was recruited by a prestigious law firm immediately afterwards. He explained that as arduous as law school had been, preparing for the bar exam would be more intense. He warned me that I wouldn't see much of him; he'd either be holed up in the study at home or at the law library poring over legal books in preparation for the exam. He'd wear a white shirt, tie, and suit every day to his new job as an associate lawyer, which was so unlike the casual clothes he'd worn to his classes. He'd bought an armful of new white shirts for the office. One day I gathered them up to wash, starch, press, and hang them in his closet. He saw me with the shirts in my arms and said, "Nell, what're you doing?"

"I'll launder your shirts," I said.

"You don't need to do that, I use the dry cleaners." He took the bundle of shirts out of my arms and threw the pile on the floor. My empty arms remained wide open as though they were missing something. He closed my arms and said, "I'd rather you put your time into this." He handed me a vanilla envelope. Inside was a collection of brochures for colleges in the area.

"Now that you have your high school degree, it's time you applied for college. That's where I want you to put your time, not cleaning and washing. And I want you and Mom to find a housekeeper who can come at least once a week.

There's a lot of people living here, you can't keep up behind the children." He took me in his arms, kissed me and said, "I love you, Nell. I want you to be as happy as I am. Let me know which colleges you want to visit." He rushed downstairs to his study.

Sometimes your mind doesn't process change and you continue to do things as you always did even when your life and world are completely different. Instinctively I felt obligated to pick up his shirts and clean them; but I flipped through the stack of college brochures instead, and walked past the dirty shirts.

# *Acknowledgments*

I started on this journey with a small group of good friends and family who were all willing to read pages and chapters of this novel as I worked away at creating the life and experiences of Nell. I thank you. Lois Lewis, Freddie Lewis Archer, Shirley Mayhew, Terry Cutler, Leslie Cutler, and my number one fan and first person to read any words I put on the page who provides edits and comments, my husband, Eric Turner. Your feedback kept me believing in the possibility that this novel would actually see the light of day and not just sit on my desk or inside the internal tangled web of my laptop.

Many thanks to my editors Alexander Weinstein for your insightful edits and suggestions about the nature of the character I was creating and for steering me in the right direction. And to Ursula DeYoung, you guided me to an ending that landed where it was meant to be.

# About the Author

JENNIFER SMITH TURNER is the author of two poetry books: *Lost and Found: Rhyming Verse Honoring African American Heroes* and *Perennial Secrets: Poetry & Prose*.

Anthony Mariel Photography

Her work has been included in *Vineyard Poets*, an anthology of poems by Martha's Vineyard writers, and in numerous literary publications. Her poems frequently appear in the *Vineyard Gazette*. She was featured on National Public Radio's *Faith Middleton Show* and Connecticut Public Television's poetry evening. She has been a featured speaker at Yale University and the University of Pennsylvania Kelly Writer's House. She has also worked extensively in the public and private K–12 schools in Connecticut and Massachusetts, bringing poetry to students and educators.

Turner formerly served as Interim President/CEO of Newman's Own Foundation, where she is a board member. She is the retired CEO of Girl Scouts of Connecticut. During her professional career, she served as an appointed government official with the State of Connecticut and the City of Hartford, as a corporate and non-profit executive, and as a member of many academic and non-profit boards of directors.

She holds a BA from Union College and a master's degree from Fairfield University. She was awarded an Honorary Doctorate of Humane Letters from the University of Hartford.

Turner resides on Martha's Vineyard with her husband, Eric.

www.jennifersmithturner.com